The Fairy Wren

Ashley Capes

For Brooke

Chapter 1

Stony Bay Books was in trouble.

Paul paced the empty floor, feather duster in hand. It had been quiet all week. Longer. All month and most of summer. He took a deep breath. His customers had gone the way of the dodo, the whisper of turning pages no longer a siren song. Even the new releases looked to be hibernating and the second-hand section up back, its shelves lined with creased spines, should have had at least one loveable nerd foraging for an obscure title. Instead it was home only to pleasant sunlight streaming in from the skylight – which, despite its pleasantness, didn't look like it was going to buy anything.

He brushed blue feathers along chest-high shelves that ran up the centre of his store, stopping at the Fantasy and Sci-Fi section. Someone had misfiled Raymond E Feist's *Magician.* Fixing it and moving on, Paul gave perfunctory swipes at the shelving. It hardly mattered. No-one was coming today either. They were obviously staying home.

Snuggling up to their e-Readers.

The doorbell chimed and he dropped the duster. "Be with you in a minute," he called, snatching the feathers up and striding to the counter, where he placed the duster out of sight. He hoped his smile was sincere. If this woman was another person asking for directions to the cinema...

"I assume you sell popular titles, young man?" She didn't bother with a greeting, instead rummaging through her voluminous handbag. Her hair was cut as if to a fashion magazine and her lipstick was an assault on his eyes.

"We sure do."

She produced a fold of paper and tossed it onto the counter.

He held her gaze until she pointed. "Well? Do you have it?"

Paul took a deep breath as he reached for the scrap. "Let's see if that one's in stock for you."

He opened the note and headed for the Thriller section. Sandra Brown. Wouldn't be too hard to find. He ran a finger along the spines as the customer tapped her foot.

"Why don't you just look it up on your computer?"

Paul kept his voice light. "Won't take a minute."

She sighed. "I have other things to do, you know."

"That's fantastic, lady," Paul whispered. "Ah, here it is," he said aloud, and pulled the title, *Deadline*, from the shelf. He returned to the insufferable woman, handing it over.

"This isn't the one I want." She gave it back with barely a glance.

"Ah, your note said *Deadline*. This is it."

She shook her head. "No. That's not right. I saw the cover, my son looked it up for me on the world wide web internet.

It has a different cover."

Paul's grip on the paperback tightened. "That might have been an overseas edition. This is the Australian cover."

"No. I want the one with the other picture." She gave the approximation of a smile. "How about you find your manager?"

"I'm the owner."

She blinked. "Well. Haven't you heard that the customer is always right?"

"I've heard that the customer is an insufferable harpy without even a rudimentary grasp on good manners, actually."

– is what he wanted to say. The woman's look of outrage almost would've made it worth losing the sale. Almost. But he couldn't afford to say it. Dennis Maddocks, gargantuan landlord of Shell Street, would soon be putting up the rent, raising it by half of where it currently stood. Both figures were a problem. The old figure was painful enough – the new one was nothing short of the foul murder of an uncle or King in true Shakespearian fashion.

Instead, he said, "Would you like me to order the overseas edition?"

She removed sunglasses from her bag and put them on. "No. I can't wait," she said, and out she walked. Paul swallowed a retort and refiled the book.

The phone rang from the counter and he dashed to it. Be a goddamn real customer, please. "Stony Bay Books, Paul speaking."

"Hello, Paul?" A young woman whispered.

"This is Paul. How can I help?"

A long pause. "Will you be at the shop for a while?"

"Ah, yeah, I will. We close at four today – did you need

me to put something aside?"

"No...I have to talk to you."

He drew half a breath, as if through water. Her voice sounded familiar, but he couldn't be sure. Her whisper was too hoarse. And *she* wasn't likely to call him. Not anymore. "Rachel?"

The line went dead.

He frowned at the receiver, as if it could provide answers. The black plastic, coated with a faint sheen of sweat, stayed predictably mute. He put the phone down and turned up the air conditioning, loosening a button on his shirt before flicking the stereo on. Herbie Hancock's *Maiden Voyage* drifted from the speakers and he leant on the counter, running a hand over the polished wood. Rachel?

Fat chance.

The intervention order had been in place for months. That still hurt, but to call him and hint at a meeting? Was she trying to trap him? Trick him into violating the terms? Just speaking to her, even if Rachel was the one to initiate contact, was a breach. It wasn't one of her friends. They'd have blasted him again over the way he'd 'treated' her. This girl, or Rachel, was acting strange. "Why all the whispering?"

"Talking to yourself again, Paul?" His uncle shuffled out of the storeroom, blue overalls and silvery hair dusted with cobwebs.

He smiled. "Seems like it. I hear it's catching."

"That sounds about right. I probably gave it to you." Henry placed a slim volume on the counter. "Here it is then, just where I said it would be. Maybe your eyes are shot, too."

"Didn't think I was that old."

"Well you're not. Wait till you get to my age."

Paul opened the book, its hardcover worn at the edges, a generous layer of dust puffing up. Inside, vibrant engravings winked up at him, reflecting the down lights. "Thanks, Henry. I really need this. Seems like it'll be one of my only sales this week."

"No worries." He cleared his throat. "So, who's whispering?" Henry was watching him carefully. Paul took the chance to talk about something else, not quite a drowning man clutching at straws, but the shoreline was distant. Realisation had been slow, honey creeping over toast, but Rachel was right. He'd been a fool for denying it so long – the store was floundering.

"I'm not sure. I got an odd phone call from a customer." He frowned. "Actually, I don't know if it was a customer at all."

"Odd how?"

"She was whispering and asking if I'd be around for a while, because she had to talk to me. She sounded worried."

"Okay."

"But she hung up. I think it was Rachel."

"You sure?"

"Not really. It could've been."

"Maybe she wants to apologise for that intervention order stunt?"

"It wasn't a stunt, Uncle Henry. I was border-line stalker there for a while." Paul shook his head at the memory of her. Turning up a few months after the breakup and jumping him. Although 'jumped' was a bit of a stretch. She'd been upset and he hadn't said no. He'd taken her hand, her skin warm beneath his fingertips... He should have walked away. Shouldn't have given her that first hug.

But she'd been shaken up.

Wouldn't talk about it after, of course, but she still had that look of worry when she'd left. He should have stopped her, found out what was wrong.

But getting slapped with an intervention order was one hell of a clear signal.

"In my day we called it fighting for the one you love," Henry said.

"She didn't see it that way."

"So is she coming over?"

"I'm not sure. If it was Rachel, she hung up, but she knows when we close."

"What's she playing at then?"

"I don't know." He glanced at his watch. Twenty minutes to four. "It's not really her style to play games, is it? She might be angry and hurt but she isn't childish."

"Well, it'll be four soon enough," Henry said as he moved round the counter and headed for the door. "And I'd better be off; I've got a party to plan."

"What? Oh, no, Henry. Please, we talked about this."

"Ah-huh."

"I feel a little sick actually. Almost flu-like."

"Really? Planning to skip out on your own birthday? Poor form, Paul." Henry grinned. "I'll see you there – don't disappoint your host now." The door closed behind him, the antique bell giving a single chime. Paul smiled as he wrapped the book in brown paper and began searching for an address.

*

Rachel, or the mystery girl, never came, though he

waited until a quarter past before shutting up shop and driving home, tapping his fingers on the steering wheel of his wagon. She was acting crazy, that was all. She didn't thrive on drama, but she wasn't above a bit of theatrics if the occasion demanded it. Once, fighting over something trivial, she'd actually tossed her head and spun away, in a movement so incredibly *Bold and the Beautiful* that they'd burst into laughter.

Traffic was light as he wound his way up the hill leading to Mayfield Drive, one of the upmarket districts overlooking the bay. Lined with green pin-oaks, whose branches stirred in the wind as he passed, it was a pleasant street. A kind of 'visitor-guide pamphlet' part of Stony Bay and far more presentable than the bilge-scum-infested water of the harbour, or the alleys with their broken glass and stench of urine. *That* would have made a novel pamphlet for tourists, maybe a Scratch-n-Sniff version – the Eastern Bay Rose Gardens, Fireman's Beach and…the Alley Behind Finnegan's Nightclub.

He pulled into his driveway and sighed, a sigh that he heaved from beneath the foot pedals. The party. Henry's intentions were good; still trying to take Paul's mind off the separation, but nothing seemed more insufferable right now. People. A crowd of them. Friends and family, drinking, laughing, eating. God. Not now. He didn't even know who was going to be there. Stepping out of the air-conditioned car, he waved to Mrs Greenhorne from across the road. She was watering her garden in a wide-brimmed straw hat, gumboots pulled up over her slacks. Mrs Greenhorne was kind enough, but he ducked into the house with his mail before she could engage him in another half-hour conversation about snail pellets and the colour of her poodle's vomit.

He'd glanced at the roof on his way in. He couldn't help it. Every time. The tiles needed cleaning. Just one more expense but at least it wasn't leaking.

Paul dumped his mail on the kitchen table and stopped, running a hand over the scratches. Her ghost wasn't in her old chair, it was in the scuff marks and grooves on the tabletop. How many meals had they shared here that first year, when all they could afford were the staples? How many bowls of spaghetti bolognaise had rested on cheap placemats, warming them through; here where he sat and watched her take such big bites, her cheeks full. His smile faded. Back then everything was certain. He'd known exactly what they both wanted. Or at least, was stupid enough to think he did.

He went to the cupboard and poured a glass of vodka, slashing it with orange juice from the fridge. He frowned as he drank. The house wasn't exactly a mess, but it needed a clean. Spots of fluff had taken over the carpet and a few cobwebs now adorned the corners of his kitchen, like thin, unwanted lace. Even the dark slate beneath his feet needed sweeping. A large crumb from last night's apple pie – *Nanna's*, he wasn't a dessert chef – proved his point. He bent to pick it up, flicking the crumb into the sink.

Housework. He made token gestures, putting a jacket away, straightening a pile of advance copies from various publishers and loading the dishwasher. The party at Henry's wasn't for two hours; he could have done more but after a while gave up and began sorting mail, separating bills and useful letters from the junk with its cheerful deals and other general life-enhancing claims. By their tone he could be forgiven for thinking that by taking up an offer, he would in fact divert the path of an oncoming meteor and save the earth.

One of the letters was from Rachel's father or 'Dr Anderson' as the man preferred. Alan's stationary suggested class and money, as befitting a well-known surgeon, as did the cream coloured envelope – it stood out from the working class white or glue-yellow used by the rest of society. The letter was typed, no doubt by an assistant, and requested that they meet 'at a time of his earliest convenience' hinting at matters of some importance.

"Come on, Alan, you couldn't just call and say what you mean?"

Paul tossed the letter into the bin.

*

Henry's home was deceptive. From the outside it looked like a typical weatherboard house with a tidy garden and veranda, even a pair of garden gnomes. Its chimney puffed smoke so lazily that the smudges barely pulled themselves up and out of the bricks. Paul wiped his feet on the welcome mat, worn down to the letters 'W' and 'E'.

A party. If only he had a clone to tag in.

He turned the handle and smothered his sigh. The interior of the house was welcoming enough, all warm wood tones, visible grain and polished surfaces. An impressive three-metre table of Blackwood dominated the dining area and the walls were lined with timber picture frames, intricate cabinets and sturdy bookshelves. Beautiful. And so familiar – as a young man, how many card games had he and his uncle played at that table, long into the night? Sometimes with Henry's daughter Mel and sometimes just the two of them.

Only now the room was packed.

Friends, old co-workers and colleagues stood with drinks in hand, conversation nearly burying Dino where he crooned from the CD player.

A round of applause and cheers greeted him. He gave a short wave before joining his uncle, neatly blocking several people who came forward. Henry stood with Mel, grinning like a fool.

"At least you didn't have everyone leap out from behind the couches and yell 'surprise'," Paul said.

Henry chuckled. "You owe Mel for that, I was going to have them do it."

"Thank you, Mel." He gave her a hug.

"You're welcome, Paul. I didn't think you needed to suffer because Dad has bad taste."

Henry chuckled. "Wait here while I get your present."

"So how's the store going?" she asked. It was an innocent enough question, but Paul knew his face gave him away. "That bad?"

"Yeah, it's been going downhill for over a year."

"God, will you have to close?"

Paul took a drink from a nearby table. Things didn't look good. He knew that. Every day he knew that. But admitting it out loud would only make it worse. Make it a betrayal. As if the store would overhear him and be hurt. Paul could see the shelves frowning at him when he walked in tomorrow. We know what you said, Paul.

He took a sip. "I don't know."

"I'm sorry to hear that."

"I'll be fine," he lied, and gave her a smile. "So you've been overseas?"

"Yeah, to the UK. England, Wales, all over. You'd love it there, Paul. The history. It's not like here where the buildings are all so young. There are keystones over there that are three times as old as our federation."

Henry returned with a wooden box, cutting off Paul's reply as he handed it over. "It's not the box, it's inside," he said.

"It looks beautiful." Paul glanced at his uncle's expectant face as he opened it, and drew a breath. Inside was a delicately carved leaf of maple, an edge curled as if picked up by the wind, its veins traceable with both eye and fingertip. Paul caught the scent of pine – though the wood was heavier than he'd been expecting.

"It's a work of art, Henry – did you carve this for me? It's amazing."

"Oh, Dad," Mel breathed.

Henry beamed. "Been working on it in the shed for months now. It's Huon Pine from Tasmania. It'll hold its scent too."

Paul embraced his uncle. "I didn't know you'd started carving again."

"Not much, but if inspiration strikes I make the time for it."

"Well, I'm obviously going to have to keep an eye on this," Paul said. "Guard it while I go to the bathroom so Mel doesn't leave with it." Mel kicked at him as he skipped out of reach.

Paul slipped into the bathroom but he didn't use the adjoining toilet, instead he leant against the basin and closed his eyes. The thud of the bass and hum of conversation was muffled and he took a few breaths.

The call nagged him. If it had been Rachel, she was jerking him round again. He could call her and find out, put a stop to whatever it was. If she answered. And if he wanted to risk a jail sentence for violating the terms of the intervention order.

He opened his phone and blinked.

Three missed calls from a private number but no messages. And he'd had the damn thing on silent.

At a knock, he shook his head. Was there no-where he could be alone a moment? "Won't be long."

Outside Jon Levitan stood smiling his dentist-assisted smile, in a half-open shirt and dark slacks. Paul noted his friend's beach-blond hair had been cut close; it seemed newly receding. "Is this where you're hiding, huh? Man of the hour, hiding in the bloody bathroom."

Paul laughed. "I needed to go." How long since he'd seen Jon? Over a month? Before the soccer club folded his friend had been around more. Last couple of years he spent a lot of time away, working hard to become a rich man. And doing a good job of it. Paul suspected their wives, who'd gone to school together, saw each other more than he and Jon did. But then, for Paul at least, that was all but 'ex-wife' now.

Jon held out a hand and for a split second, his smile became strained. Paul shook his friend's hand and the smile eased. Had he imagined the strain?

"Thirty-four. How does it feel?" Jon asked.

"Remarkably similar to thirty three years and three hundred and sixty four days."

"Well, well, aren't you a funny guy? I suppose you're going to tell me –" A dance-song tore through Jon's pocket. He pulled his phone, a sleek black device that was no doubt cutting edge, and switched it off. "Sorry about that, I'll call them back. Bloody builders and deadlines." Jon had his fingers – no, his whole arms – in several pies, construction, housing investments and even an interest in an A League Soccer Club.

"So, you tried to call me yesterday?"

"Yes I did, Birthday Boy." He glanced around. "Here, I wanted to ask you something." He herded Paul back into the bathroom and closed the door, which he then leant on. Jon lowered his voice. "I have something you'll be interested in. A bit of a business proposition."

Paul gave him a look. "Do you? And we have to discuss it in the bathroom?"

"It's a quiet place," Jon shrugged. "Anyway, here it is. I need your help to write off one of my cars."

"What?"

"Just wait. I've figured it all out, you'd get something for it and –"

"No way," Paul cut him off. He strode to the door and glared until Jon moved aside.

"Think about it."

"No thanks," Paul said as returned to the party, letting the chatter and music envelop him. Jon didn't follow but he'd try again; he was a persistent guy. One of Jon's virtues, if it could be called that. But it was a bloody stupid idea. Paul shook his head. The party. He had to make at least a bit of an effort tonight. Moving around the room, he tried to chat with everyone at least once, but found himself eyeing the door.

Sarah Jennings, former employee and proud mother approached, and he became the Titanic facing a moving iceberg. A sickeningly sympathetic expression covered her face – she was no doubt eager to gossip, and he couldn't escape without deliberately turning from her.

"Sarah." He gave her a hug and she returned it with one arm, the other occupied with a glass of wine, which she held like a dance partner. "How is Benjamin? He must be four or five by now?"

"Four," she said, but his attempt to engage a natural inclination to boast about her son was useless. There was 'sympathy' to be dispersed. "Oh, you poor thing, I haven't seen you since Rachel left. Are you doing okay?"

"Miserable at times. Relieved at others. It's confusing and painful," he said, hoping some honesty would shorten the conversation. It almost worked, but Sarah recovered quickly.

"I hear she's shacked up with the Mayor Dolan's son, Grady."

"How civic of her." It was news to him.

"Yes, people think they might be getting engaged soon. He certainly seems smitten. He's into the stock market, you know."

"You don't say? Maybe he should consult the previous owner before he invests," Paul tried, but she prattled on and it became like a boxing match. He attempted to knock her gossip aside with short, curt, and even more absurd answers, but she had more than a few punches to throw and didn't seem to be listening to his responses. She wasn't malicious, just hopelessly misguided. Sarah probably thought he needed to talk about it. To see how Rachel was moving on, to show him it was okay if he did too. But he didn't. To put Rachel from his mind was what he needed. But ten years weren't that easy to file away.

"...and now she's taken up gardening and she's looking

for a position at one of the nurseries. Apparently she has her eye on Franklin's Garden Supplies."

Paul nodded. She was actually fairly good in the garden. Aloud, he said, "That's good to hear, but I'd better be off now, Sarah. I've had a long day, you know?" He took her hand, cutting her goodbye short as he slipped by.

Finding Henry, he collected his gift, thanked his uncle again and made his farewells, allowing Mel to shove a piece of cake into his mouth. Henry's face fell when Paul announced he was leaving early, but another minute of tedious small talk and he'd vomit. "Delicious," he tried to say through the cake, managing another to wave to the crowd from the door.

Henry followed Paul outside, catching his shoulder. "Did Rachel show up?"

He swallowed, the sweetness churning his stomach. "No. I guess it was a mistake. Someone called me again though. Three times."

"It's her, Paul. Call her back."

Paul's slow nod finished up a shake of the head. "Maybe. If it was her. And if I want to go to jail, or cop a fine which I can't afford."

"Well, think about it," Henry said. "If you two are meant to be together you should try. Believe me, Paul, you don't want to make the same mistake I did with Patsy."

Paul put his free hand on Henry's shoulder. "You did everything you could. You got help, she could have stayed."

Henry gave a wry smile. "I didn't do it quick enough, though, did I? You should call her. And sooner rather than later, fancy intervention order or not."

"I will think about it."

"Good." Henry waved him off.

The moon beamed down on Paul, bright enough to illuminate the path and the wheelie-bin standing on the curb. It was like a vaguely unpleasant valet waiting to escort him down the line of vehicles, which were in turn, patient and mute as they waited for their drivers. His own car was parked some distance away; he'd purposefully arrived late enough so that he wasn't boxed in. Once inside, he put the maple leaf in its box on the passenger seat and leant back a moment, closing his eyes.

He should stay longer, for Henry. Go back in, make some stupid joke about needing air. Apologise. Especially after all the work his uncle had put in. Not just the gift, but the food, opening up his home and organising the guests. Some of them people Paul hadn't seen for a long time.

No. Henry meant well, and so did Mel and probably even Jon, but the others? How many were there simply to get some good, first hand gossip? Separated for months and people still couldn't stop talking about it. They'd probably want to discuss the store too. Corner him with their treacly expressions. And the intervention order. Didn't they just love that?

Better to get out and slam his hand in the door.

Chapter 2

Someone was knocking on his door. They didn't seem able to accept that he didn't mean to get up. The knocking continued and he groaned, rolling over. Seven am? Sunday had lost all of its holiness. Day of Rest indeed. Whoever was knocking was evil, surely evil to their rotten core. If only he were a religious fellow – he'd petition God to strike them down.

"Mr Fischer? Are you home? Mr Fischer, please, it's important!"

Mrs Greenhorne's voice was strained. Paul stood, fumbling for his dressing gown where it hung on the door to his walk-in wardrobe. He groaned and cinched it tight, not wanting to offend her, even though he slept in boxer shorts.

"I'm coming," he called as he lumbered down the hall. The knocking stopped just as he opened the door to the rising sun. Mrs Greenhorne, looking quite prim with her shawl and hat, stood on his doorstep, her arm around a girl of about twelve. With her tanned complexion and black hair, the girl might have been Greek or maybe Italian. Her face was smudged with dirt and deep circles ringed her eyes. While her jeans were designer, they were ragged at the edges and she fidgeted as she looked around. A rumpled bag sat on the concrete step and she stood over it in a protective stance.

"Good morning," he rasped, then cleared his throat, feeling a flash of guilt when the girl flinched.

"I must apologise for waking you, Mr Fischer," Mrs Greenhorne began. "But this girl woke me earlier and I think she needs help but I have an appointment. Heather next door isn't home and I wondered if you could help?"

"Has anything happened?"

"I really don't know, she just seems...lost. I asked where her parents were but I don't know if she understood."

Paul wished he were wearing proper clothes, but he smiled in what he hoped was a friendly manner. "Hi. Are you lost? Can I call someone for you maybe?"

She said nothing.

"I should get back to Eddie, we're running late." Mrs Greenhorne glanced back at her house. Through the vertical blinds Paul could see her son seated at their table; the man had cerebral palsy and had been confined to a wheelchair all his life. Paul guessed it was a medical appointment of some sort. She looked back to the girl. "Her name is Alessandra and she's here from Italy – I suspect that much, but I doubt she speaks English."

"Hi, Alessandra, my name is Paul." He smiled again. "*Sono* Paul." He tried to recall more of his high school Italian, but there wasn't much there. He probably screwed up the accent too.

"Paul," she said, staring up at him.

"Where did she come from?" he asked Mrs Greenhorne.

"I've no idea, Mr Fischer, but I really must go," she said, and was off, clutching her handbag. He looked at Alessandra. What now? "Are you thirsty?" he said after a moment. She made no response and he tried again. "*L'Aqua?*"

She nodded, collected her bag and followed him inside. He'd probably have to call the Department of Human Services. Or better, the police, to see if there were any runaways. Maybe even visit Battisti's bakery. Anton would be able to talk to her. Getting the girl a glass of water, he gestured for her to sit at the table. He pulled a chair and sat across from her with his own glass. When she was finished, Alessandra produced a photo from her pocket, glanced at it and put it away. It was black and white but he caught a glimpse.

"Who's that?" He pointed to the picture.

She showed him but didn't let it out of her hand. "Anita."

Anita was a beautiful young woman, smiling but looking away from the camera. By her clothing, the image looked to be well over twenty years old. "Is that your mother?" he asked, not able to remember Italian for 'mother' for some reason.

She said nothing, only putting the picture away and glancing at the front door.

"Are you hungry?" he asked. "Ah…" He mimed eating.

Alessandra shook her head, reeled off a couple of phrases in Italian and fell quiet again. "How about I get you something to eat anyway?" he said after another long moment of silence. "Then I can call someone for you, how about that?" He couldn't remember any more Italian, he'd been a poor student of language, and she didn't seem to know any English. Paul got up and rummaged through his pantry. "How about chocolate?" he asked without turning. All he found was an old box of imported *Junior Mints*, Rachel's favourite – but it was empty and Alessandra didn't answer. No chocolate then. "*Biscotti?*" Still nothing. He slid some jars around and found a packet of dried fruit, apricots and bananas among other things that should never be dried, but passed it over. "What about ice cream?"

Alessandra was gone.

He called her name and searched the house but by the time he realised the front door was not fully closed, it was too late. He checked the road, still in his robe, ignoring the looks he got from the occasional passing driver. Gone.

*

Once dressed and composed, Paul filed reports with both the police and the Department, supplying them with his and Mrs Greenhorne's addresses. There wasn't much else he could do. Maybe she was a runaway, maybe not. Stony Bay wasn't exactly overflowing with Italian tourists, but it wasn't beyond the realm of possibility that she was visiting and had wandered off from somewhere. Maybe it was an overreaction, but reporting it was the right thing to do. She was just a child. Abductions happened. Even in 'nice' places like Stony Bay.

Paul attempted to resume his day. He couldn't even remember what he'd planned. Housework? Dusting his groaning bookshelves? The one in the hall wore the look of an overfed, smug pet, content to wait him out and the two in the lounge were no better. Instead he paced. He tapped out an uneven beat on the bench top. He ate half a bowl of cereal, peeled a banana and got several bites in before binning it.

The private number from last night was still a mystery, but that didn't mean it wasn't Rachel. She could have changed her number, she could have been calling from another phone. Or it could have been a telemarketer. Maybe violating his intervention order to call her was worth the risk, just to see if she answered?

He grabbed his phone. Another missed call.

Jon.

Might as well get it over with. It was one phone call at least, that he was permitted by law to make. Paul dialled and waited. His friend didn't pick up and he hung up before voicemail clicked in. He tried again and this time Jon answered, voice sounding bright. "Paul. Hope I didn't wake you before?"

"I was up."

"You sound grumpy there."

"Do I? I'm not. About last night –"

"It's fine. I looked for you, but you left kind of early."

Paul had to smile. He hadn't been about to apologise. "Yeah. Well, I didn't really want to hear any more about your scam."

"You sure about that?"

"Yep."

A moment of silence. "How about we have lunch then, just a bit of a catch up?"

Paul rubbed his neck. "All right. Where are we eating?"

*

Once again Jon wore slacks and a button up shirt open at the throat, displaying a little of his sculpted chest. He'd chosen a fancy restaurant, *the nouveau* – all lowercase – with black tablecloths and crystal vases and tasselled menus. The place was crowded and Paul barely noticed the muzak sagging from the speakers, strategically placed in the crooks of walls or nestled beside giant, abstract canvases. Instead he was attempting to digest the prices. Quietly and without making strange faces.

"I hope you're paying."

"Exactly what I want to hear from a prospective business partner," Jon said, and winked at the waitress, who stood in her black and white outfit, pen on pad. Paul thought she almost rolled her eyes, and only the barest of shivers marred the line of her shoulders. Jon ordered whisky and Paul asked for vodka and orange.

"Business partner?" Paul sighed. Catching up would have been great but he'd been waiting for it. "Jon –"

His friend held up his hands. "I'm not trying to force you but I think you should listen to me at least. I know the store isn't going so well. I recognise the signs. You going to tell me you couldn't use some help? And believe me, this is rock-solid."

Paul said nothing. He *could* use the money. Hated admitting it, but it was true. He'd been staring at that truth for a long while now. But it wasn't worth it.

"Come on. Nothing will go wrong."

"You don't know that. It's an insurance scam," Paul said. "Not rock-solid at all."

Jon frowned. "It's a way for you to get a bit of breathing room, Paul. Listen a minute. I only need you to steal my

Mustang and write it off – that's it. Nothing else, you don't need to meet with anyone, no-one needs to know you're even involved. Just me, just like we used to do."

"Used to? I was an unwitting driver back then, Jon. Shit, I didn't even know what was going on until after."

"True, but this time you can actually get something for your troubles. Come on."

He gulped down his drink. "Thanks, Jon, but I don't think so." He left the table, ignoring the man's hissing pleas.

Once outside the restaurant, he slumped against his car, shaking. It wasn't cold and he wasn't angry. Or so he tried to tell himself. And he wasn't tempted. At all. Things weren't so bad that he had to resort to – he jumped when a hand fell on his shoulder, the traffic having concealed Jon's footsteps. "Paul. Just hear the rest. I can help you with the shop. You've let me help you before, come on."

"Not like this, I didn't." Paul shook his head and slipped into the driver's seat. "I'm not doing that."

"I can't trust anyone else." Jon caught Paul's wrist before he could turn the key.

"Don't you mean you wouldn't have leverage over anyone else?"

His mouth thinned into a line and he let go. "No. I don't mean that. And that's not fair at all. I've never done that to you, Paul. Not once. Not with the roof. Not with the operation, not ever. You know that."

Paul sighed. He was right. When things were tough, at the store or otherwise, Jon was there. It'd been that way since they were kids. "Yeah, I know. I'm sorry." He fired the engine. "But I can't."

"It's your future."

"I know." He pulled out of the car park, merging with traffic, fists tight on the wheel as he headed toward Mayfield Drive. It *was* his future and it wasn't looking good.

Pulling into his driveway, Paul stomped on the brake. A tiny bird with brilliant blue feathers swooped down to land before his grill, its head giving a single twitch as it regarded him. Its eyes were liquid-like, tracking his car as he eased forward. He expected the creature to fly, or at least hop away, but it didn't look like it was going to shift so he stopped and got out. With careful steps, he moved to the front of the car and bent down, stomach tightening.

The bird chirped at him, unperturbed by the tonne of Mitsubishi wagon resting over it. Small enough that it wasn't in danger from the car, the bird was calm, despite his closeness. Paul almost reached out a hand, encouraged by its placidity, but the slight movement caused the bird to take a single, rather deliberate step backward.

It nuzzled beneath a wing for a moment, then drew forth something silver with its beak, dropping it on the ground with a small clink.

Paul drew a breath.

His wedding band sat on the concrete. The ring he'd thrown into the backyard. Hurled at the back fence actually. Months ago. He'd regretted it later, more so when he realised he couldn't find it again.

No cameras seemed to be watching him; no kids were holding remote consoles and pointing, faces bright with glee, Mrs Greenhorne was not in her garden, her son not peering through the dining window. The strange guy from two doors down was not by the water-meter and no goofy host was approaching with a wind-sock microphone to tell him how stupid he looked.

The bird was gone when he looked back, but he heard a chirping from the garage roof and turned just in time to see it flit from sight.

Chapter 3

Paul walked Mayfield Drive. He was shirtless, his feet bare. The strips of pyjama pants fluttered round his legs. He should have been afraid but the wind was sweet against his chest. It was dark. Moonlight hit the tar in spots, some large, some small, as though the clouds had been turned into Swiss cheese. He paused among them, letting the light whisper against his eye-lids.

Houses were sleeping. Lawns were side-sleeping. Flowers had been chloroformed. Paul giggled and the notes he made slipped from his fingers and shattered on the ground. He knelt, and careful not to cut himself, scooped them up with a nearby shirt, one that appeared with wonderful fortuitousness.

In his makeshift cradle of cloth the pieces melted together, growing warm. He blew on them until they caught fire, pale blue flames that did not rise too high. Inside were scattered words, moving restless and tense, as if hard at work on musical chairs. The blue-flame words soon engulfed his hands and became so heavy that he had to drop them, where they burst into feathers and twisted into a giant, writhing bird, one that hulked up and stretched out, becoming twice his size in the time it took him to blink.

Then it reached out with massive wings, opened its beak and engulfed him.

*

Paul woke, sweat dampening twisted sheets. It was well into the night – his room was full of it – and it seemed to lie across him in heavy clumps. His bedside clock was a beacon, steady green glow spelling out the numbers for two in the morning. He barely remembered crawling into bed, or much before it. Walking inside after the blue bird, marvelling at his ring while he ate some lunch, and finally falling asleep in front of the television was about it. At some point he must have dragged himself to bed. It might have explained the hungry rumblings in his stomach, and since something urgent was happening in his bladder, he stumbled to the toilet.

In the kitchen he made himself toast, chomping down four slices with slabs of butter, before returning to bed. His wedding ring rested by the lamp. Crazy. How did the bird know where it was? An odd feeling battered its way through the haze. Something big was supposed to happen tomorrow. He couldn't remember what it was but the sense of expectation slept with him, like an undercurrent or a particularly benign case of tinnitus. The feeling remained when he woke a few hours later and hummed his way through a quick breakfast of banana and orange juice. It stayed with him on the way to the store, tapping away in fingers on the steering wheel as they kept the beat to 'Cantaloupe Island,' in the slam of his door in the alley behind Shell Street, and its gravelly echo too. The click of the lock and the urn, the jingle of the till and the muted swoosh of blinds being opened in the kitchenette. It stayed with him, a kind of invisible parrot on his shoulder, right up until he saw Teddy Prendergast at the door.

Then it took flight in a shower of tingling feathers.

Today he was to meet with Stony Bay's very own real estate tycoon, the Grinch of Shell Street. Dennis Maddocks. Teddy waved.

"Come in, Teddy." Paul unhooked the chain and flicked the lock open, returning to the counter as the tall man followed him inside.

"Thanks, Paul. I was starting to wonder if you were going to make it in today. If you'd forgotten. You know, today's the big day, right?" His voice was high-pitched, not quite a match for his build.

"Right."

"It's just that you were a little late today. It's nearly nine-thirty."

Paul began to count his small change. "I haven't forgotten, Teddy," he said between the five and ten cent trays.

"Good, because we're all counting on you, you know. I left Trish on the till to come here and give you this; it's the final draft of the letter. Did you want to read over it? Thing is, we've already sent it to Maddocks and the Agent," he mumbled.

"I'm sure it's all there, Teddy," he said. "Just leave it with me." He gave the man what he hoped was a reassuring smile, accepted the letter and stopped counting to usher Teddy to the door. "I'm going to do my best. You know I think someone else should be speaking for us, but I will do my best."

Teddy looked over his shoulder. This close, the worry lines were even more pronounced. The man looked a little grey beneath the eyes and he licked his lips before giving another nod. "Thanks, Paul. Call us when you're done. I know that Albert especially is sailing close to the wind, you know?"

"I do."

Once Teddy left, Paul began adjusting the new releases in the window. It needed to be Windexed but instead he lost himself in the work of arranging covers, trying to guess which titles, authors and artworks would draw people in. A new Stephen King novel might have done it, but there wasn't one. Even better would have been a Harry Potter title.

He ignored the letter where it sat on his register; he ignored it when he accepted a delivery later that morning; when he passed it on his way to the kitchen for coffee and whenever he answered the phone. He'd been expecting Rachel to call but wasn't going to contact her. The order was crystal clear on that one, and besides, if she really wanted to talk, she could be the one to make contact. And properly this time.

Despite various telemarketers, one call at least was meaningful. His Uncle Henry was going to send Mel to fill in – Paul needed someone to watch the books meditate in their shelves during his meeting. He could have closed up, but lunch was the best time of day for customers. Not that it was ever a rush.

"Thanks, Henry. Are you all right?"

"Just a bit under the weather. Nothing to worry about,"

he paused. "Have you heard from Rachel?"

"No. And I don't know if I will. Maybe she was drunk."

"Could be. Let me know if you decide to call her."

"I will. Get some rest too, and tell Mel the appointment is at one."

"All right. Good luck with that snake Maddocks."

By the time Mel arrived, he'd boxed half his returns, rearranged a small sale table by the counter and repriced nearly a shelf's worth of books. He had a series of 'Staff-Pick' cards ready to place beside 'high-profile' books but hadn't put them out, seeing as he was, officially at least, the only 'Staff.' One of his picks was *Paprika* by Yasutaka Tsutsui but he hadn't figured out what to write on it. Recommended for light sleepers?

"The store looks great," Mel said, taking off a pair of chunky sunglasses and looking around. She grinned. "Much cleaner than last time I visited."

"Surprising, the amount of work that can be done when no-one's around." He smiled, hoping it looked wry rather than bitter. His only customer so far was a pensioner who stole a four-pack of batteries from the counter while he was searching the back room for a title that she requested, and politely declined when he finally produced it.

"A bit slow today?"

"Yeah, though they're out there," he said, looking through the windows into the busy street. The passage of people was not unlike a fleshy train speckled with colourful fabric. Maybe he needed Velcro pads near the front door? "Why don't you put your bag in the back? There's coffee out there too if you like — it's only instant though."

"I can stomach it."

"Seen this kinda register before?"

"Close to. When I worked for Myer." Mel walked around to stand behind the counter.

He took a breath. "Is your dad all right?"

"Just a bit tired from the party," she said, her voice even.

"I shouldn't have left so early."

Mel shook her head. "He'll be all right, Paul, but he was upset."

He looked away. "I'll apologise after this damn meeting. I should have stayed."

"He'd like that – but don't tell him I said anything."

He took the letter. "I won't. Back around two."

"Deal."

Both sides of Shell Street were stuffed with pedestrians, in the way that it always was this time of year, with local people who looked both familiar and annoyed, and people with the tourist stamp – carefree, lazily dressed and always eating. He pushed through them without too much jostling; passing the Battisti Bakery, Teddy's fishing shop, Albert's impeccably clean fruit shop and a good half dozen cafes. The centre strip of grass and evenly spaced trees, manicured to their green cuticles, were home to bench seats, tradesmen and office folk eating rolls and pies, along with the odd seagull scouting for scraps. Cars cut laps round the strip looking for the oasis of the CBD, the parking space, and an argument erupted over a good spot right in front of Stony Bay Real Estate.

Ignoring the quarrelling men, he slipped into the agency and alerted the vapid receptionist to his presence by clearing his throat. She blinked. "Oh, hello Mr Fischer. How are you today?"

"Good, Jenny. I'm here to see Kelly Wilson and Dennis Maddocks, if they're ready?"

"I'll check." She picked up a phone, dialled, spoke to Kelly Wilson, one of the property managers, and sent him through once she had confirmation. "Second one on the right, down that hall."

"Thank you."

At the door he paused a second before opening it. He wasn't the right guy for the job but everyone was depending on him, he couldn't let them down with a half-arsed performance. Stand up to the big guys or get wiped out, Paul, don't waste this opportunity. He was no Robin Hood of Small Business but this was their big chance to meet with the Grinch. After all, the man had 'spared them' some time, as Kelly told him, the hint of an apology in her voice.

Maddocks was the worst kind of weekender – the kind that milked a community to expand business interests in a distant city, before buying a place in the same community in order to be seen 'spending weekends on the coast.'

Kelly looked up from where she sat across from Dennis Maddocks. She wore a tight grey suit with a white shirt that allowed a glimpse of her cleavage. Her dark hair was pulled into a professional pony tail and her studs were business-like silver. She looked a career woman, no doubt about it. "Thanks for coming, Paul." Her smile was obviously meant to bolster his spirits. Bad sign.

"Good afternoon to you both," he said as he joined her, setting himself opposite Maddocks. The aging man gave a nod, glancing at his watch, which looked to be a Rolex. Paul nearly laughed. The ultimate in status symbols. Sure, it was accurate – the guy was a rich, rich man. But it was almost as clichéd as his suit, slicked back hair or the insufferably bored expression. The man was a hack.

Kelly opened proceedings with her 'bright voice', the one he'd heard her use when speaking on the phone to a prospective client. "Mr Maddocks was telling me that he hasn't had a chance to read your request. Are you able to summarise it for him?"

"I can." Paul controlled a frown by looking down to the envelope, opening and glancing at the letter. It was fairly emotive stuff, more than a few retailers' livelihoods were at stake and he knew for one, medical treatment might soon be out of reach. He said as much and finished simply. "Basically, we're asking you to hold off on the rent rise if possible, Mr Maddocks. Even for the next six months – it would help us greatly; give us a chance to consolidate our customer base in order to better cope with the rise."

Dennis Maddocks waited for him to finish before answering, waving a hand. "I understand what you're all saying, Fischer. I do. But costs are rising everywhere. For me as a developer and as an owner. It's not something I can put off forever, you know."

Like hell you can't. Paul made to reply but Kelly opened her copy of the letter, which he knew she'd already read. "The retailers also asked if it were possible to lessen the rise at this stage. Is that something you'd be in a position to consider?"

Maddocks shot her an angry look before turning back to Paul. "No. That wouldn't be feasible, I'm sorry to say."

The conversation stalled after that, with Maddocks giving similarly polite rebuttals to similarly phrased requests for the same concessions. Throughout, Paul gripped the arms of his chair and kept his breathing even. Finally Kelly called it to a close, seeing the man out of the room. Paul followed, muscles strained, stomach churning. Kelly rested a hand on his arm. "Still want me to take you to lunch, Paul?"

"No, thank you, Kelly. I know you tried in there. Appreciate it." Keeping his tone polite was a struggle.

"I understand –"

"Thanks again." Storming past Jenny's desk; he flung the door open and burst onto the footpath, turning down the alley beside the offices and kicking at a bag of rubbish. It went a little way toward making him feel better but it wasn't enough. He swore beneath his breath as he walked, finding himself in the car park. Polished vehicles were lined up between neat white lines. One of them had to be Maddocks'. Maybe he'd kick a panel in, see how the man liked that. He started toward a silver Mercedes, it had to be the Grinch's, when a blue bird alighted on a nearby Land Cruiser.

It chirped down at him, head bobbing.

He stopped. Was it the same bird, the one that found his ring? Didn't seem likely. It continued to chirp, agitation clear as it hopped on the spot. He frowned. The chirping was distinctly disapproving...

Before he could move closer, the door to Stony Bay Real Estate squeaked open. The bird leapt into flight, disappearing as laughter preceded two men. It was Maddocks and another suit – one of the big-wigs of the agency, a greying man whose name Paul had never caught. "We can probably have some of the businesses out by the end of next month if they can't keep up," the man was saying.

"Earlier would be better," Maddocks said.

Bastards, the both of them.

"We'll see, Dennis." The agent shook Maddocks' hand

and went back inside, leaving the Grinch to walk to his car.

"What are you doing here, Fischer?"

"Were you ever going to listen to us?" Blood surged through his veins.

"Look, buddy. This is business, you got it? If you think you can stick around out back and convince me, pull on my heart strings, then you're wrong." He sneered. "I've got so many new managers wanting a piece of Shell Street that I hardly need you lot. These businesses are willing to pay twice what you do and they're ready to move in now. It's not personal. Whoever can pay stays, doesn't matter to me."

"Did you read the letter, because –"

"Hey," he snapped, taking a step forward. "Get a clue, pal! I don't give a fuck about you people, I don't care who's dying, how many of you might go broke; it doesn't mean shit. You're walking dollar signs to me, got it?" He punctuated his words by jabbing his finger into Paul's chest. "Now get out of my way, Fischer."

Paul stiffened. He might have let it go before this display, but being prodded? No way. His voice went quiet. "Not rich enough yet, you stupid prick?"

Dennis Maddocks' face went red and he began poking at Paul again, hollering at the top of his lungs. "What did you say, you little bastard, I'll –"

Paul caught the man's hand and twisted his arm, shoving the property developer up against the car and pushing until Maddocks let out a shout. "Do that with your finger again and I'll break it off, Dennis."

"Let me go." The man spat.

Paul increased the pressure, watching the Grinch squirm for a good minute before releasing him. Maddocks staggered, rubbing his arm as he swore. His face was white now and he heaved in air around his words. "You're dead meat, Fischer – I'll crush you now. I'll take your store and then I'll take you for everything you've got. Assault, you dumbshit. Once my lawyers are through with you, you won't have twenty fucking cents to your name."

Hiding behind his money. Fucking typical. "I'd better make it worthwhile then." Paul stepped in and delivered a punch that snapped the real estate tycoon's head back, the crack of his jaw echoing around the car park. Maddocks collapsed against his Mercedes, slumping to the ground, his eyes glazed.

Paul walked away, doing his best not to imagine the cheers of a non-existent crowd.

Chapter 4

Paul had let Mel go early, telling her a very short version of events and closing up shop before driving over to see Toshiro, his old Jeet Kune Do instructor.

Or at least, that was the plan.

Only Toshiro wasn't home, and neither was Henry when Paul checked. And so, having no-one else, he drove the streets, replaying the confrontation. The crack of the punch echoed in his mind and he grinned. Felt pretty bloody good to hit the bastard, too bad he couldn't do it again.

Paul snorted at his reflection in the rear-view mirror. Idiot. Maddocks would probably come after Teddy and the others too now, because it would hurt Paul more, to be responsible for that.

Finally he tried Henry again. This time his uncle was home and Paul started with an apology about the party. Henry gave a nod of acceptance then raised his eyebrows when he learnt about Paul's outburst. "Good. Got what he deserved, the bastard," he said, slapping the kitchen bench.

"Only, I'm probably in for some of the same," Paul said.

"Legally, anyway."

"Call that lawyer of your father's," Henry said.

"Lloyd?"

"Can't hurt."

It wasn't a bad idea; he needed help. "Thanks, Henry."

Dark had well and truly fallen when Paul got home, rushing through the night ritual of closing blinds and turning on lights. Leaning on the old mantle where he'd placed Henry's carving, he ordered pizza before putting on *Kind of Blue*. A hot shower would have been nice but he couldn't be bothered and didn't want to miss the delivery.

Maddocks. That filthy prick.

By the time he'd finished visiting Teddy, Albert and the other retailers, he was exhausted. Most of them had expected to be turned down; they knew the Grinch's reputation. He'd done it before. Albert wrung his hands but offered fierce congratulations upon hearing that Paul had punched the Grinch. Lydia Sanders from the health shop called him a moron and accused him of ruining their lives, unable or unwilling to hear him when he explained that Maddocks had always meant to force them out.

"She'll figure it out," he told the television remote.

A knock startled him. "I'm on my way," he shouted, and found some money before rushing to open the door. "That was quick, I was..." he trailed off. Kelly from Stony Bay Real Estate stood on his front step, still in her work clothes.

"Paul, I've been trying to call you for hours."

"Kelly, I'm sorry, come in. I thought you were the pizza guy." He led her to the kitchen table. "Is something wrong?" How could there not be? He'd never had a property manager visit him late at night, and considering what he'd done earlier...

"Ah, if your name is still Paul Fischer, then yes, something is wrong. Maddocks isn't happy. Before he left for his solicitor, he told Martin that he'd crush you."

"Just me?"

She raised an eyebrow. "Someone else hit him in the car park too?"

"I just don't want him going after the others."

"Oh. I don't think so." A silence began to stretch, and Kelly glanced at him. "Paul, I came here tonight to warn you."

"About the Grinch? Thanks, Kelly, but I knew he'd come after me. I think I knew when I swung."

"But it didn't stop you."

He gave a slow shrug. Strangely enough, it didn't seem odd to be talking with her about things a property manager shouldn't know. "No. For some reason it didn't."

"Well I kinda came here to warn you about Martin Roberts, my boss. He's gunning for you too, now. He and Dennis Maddocks are old friends."

"Great." Just what he needed. Another angry rich man looking to settle the score.

He caught Kelly staring at him again, and saw her properly for the first time since she'd walked in. Her shirt revealed more of her breasts than was entirely professional. She looked good, her skin smooth. Her pony tail was still tied up, but her eye-shadow looked fresh and she had no briefcase, just a handbag. Her skirt hugged her hips as she moved to the CD player and picked up the Miles Davis case.

"I never really liked jazz," she said.

"It took me a while." He was getting short of breath.

What was happening here? Kelly had never looked at him twice before now. She was a little younger than him and probably out of his league, the kind of confident woman who would no doubt be in a happy relationship. When she twisted the CD case he saw that she wore no ring. His pulse quickened, like a gear had shifted in his head. It was surprisingly smooth, for a machine that hadn't been out of the mechanic's workshop for a while. Since Rachel all those months ago, he hadn't slept with anyone. The store had taken too much of his time and he'd been busy with –

Kelly stood before him. "Paul, I was thinking. I've had a pretty long day and I came straight from the office...I hope this doesn't sound rude, but I heard you mention pizza?"

He caught the cue. Well done, Paul. "Would you like to stay for dinner?"

"If it's not too much trouble?"

"No, that'd be good," he said. "How about I pour us a drink?"

"I could use a coffee actually." She looked around the room. "And I wouldn't mind freshening up a little?"

"Bathroom's down the hall, second on the left," Paul said over his shoulder, hands busy with the coffee machine, or shaking before it, if he was honest. He wanted her, though he hadn't realised it before tonight. Did that even make sense? Maybe he'd never felt the need before now. By the time Kelly returned to the table, he'd made the drinks and had half his cup, managing to get his hands under control. Not that she took her time, but he was drinking fast, despite the hot coffee. "Milk but no sugar, right?"

She smiled. "How did you know that?"

"I've heard you give that order to Jenny at the office."

"Ah." She took a sip and gave a nod to herself.

Another moment of silence fell between them. *Flamenco Sketches* was coming to an end and then it would just be the mouse-like sounds of the house itself or the sounds their cups made whenever they were set down.

"I'm glad you hit Maddocks. I saw his jaw. Do you do weights or something?"

He flushed. "I kinda do a bit of martial arts."

Her eyes lit up. "Really?" He watched her and fancied he actually saw the moment she made her decision. She stood and walked around the table. "What could you show me then, Paul?"

He pulled her close. "Some things." He undid one of her buttons, then another, sucking in a breath when he found that she'd removed her bra. When did she do that? He leant forward to trail his tongue across her skin and heard her murmur something about his bed.

"Which way?"

He pointed and she led him from the kitchen.

*

Kelly was gone when his alarm roared into life; an ad where the announcer screamed his guts out about the savings at Harris Scarfe, which Paul flicked off with a growl, but there was a note on the kitchen table. In her happy-looking handwriting waited her house phone and the word 'Kelly' with an 'X' beneath it. He placed the note in his wallet. Maybe they'd gone a little fast, but then, Rachel hadn't exactly taken her time with the Mayor's son.

Paul found a second note on the doorstep when he checked for the paper, this being from a rather disgruntled pizza delivery service.

He didn't even remember hearing the bell.

Mrs Greenhorne and her son were in their yard. She was gardening in gloves, gumboots and some sort of outdoor apron. Eddie was simply enjoying the sunshine. Her poodle sat in a patch of shade, wagging its puff-ball tail. Paul waved to them, and she laid her secateurs aside, waving back. "Mr Fischer, might I speak with you a moment?"

He crossed the street. "Good morning, Mrs Greenhorne. Hey, Eddie."

"Hi, Paul, how are you going?" Eddie said, speaking with some difficulty, but not so much that Paul couldn't follow. He'd had more than enough conversations with Eddie over the years to understand him just fine.

"Very good, actually. How about you?" While he did feel good, very good indeed after Kelly's visit, there was no point going into detail about the hell that he was probably going to face with Dennis Maddocks. For now, he could ignore that, and Eddie wouldn't want to hear about it anyway. Who would?

"Good. I've been writing more music, you can come and hear some if you like?"

"Yeah, I'd like that – how about in a couple of nights?"

"Wonderful." Mrs Greenhorne smiled down at her son. "He's so good with that computer of his," she said. "It's like another world to me though. In any event, I thought I should tell you, I saw that girl again, yesterday."

"Who?"

"Alessandra. The runaway. She came up to your house, knocked and looked around a bit before leaving. She even smelled those roses you have in the front garden, sad little things. I called to her but she didn't answer."

"Really?" The streets were certainly empty of strange Italian pre-teens now. Only the morning traffic flowed by, their shiny rooftops reflecting leaf patterns from the oak branches. "I meant to ask you, do you know where she came from?"

"No, she just turned up, holding that photo of hers. Anita is probably her mother, don't you think? They certainly look alike."

"But she was back yesterday?"

"Around lunchtime, I'd say."

"Yeah, lunchtime," Eddie added.

Paul frowned. "If you see her again, it's probably worth calling the police. I don't think she's dangerous –"

"Nor I," Mrs Greenhorne interjected.

"– but she's obviously lost. Maybe she's looking for her mother?"

"Of course. I did inform the police today, and they eventually drove by but I haven't heard from them since. Such a small police force, really. Probably overworked too."

Paul looked up Mayfield Drive. "Does anyone in the street have Italian relatives staying over?"

"Oh no, not that I'm aware of. I made a few calls."

Paul held back a smile. No doubt she had, to every gossip in town. "Well, I guess there's not much else we can do. I'd better finish breakfast and get down to the store."

He was a little late again, but no-one was waiting at the door this time, and so he set up a few stands, got a couple dozen copies of the new John Grisham in a display and took the mail to the counter. Spliced between junk was a note from the post office; he had a package waiting at Tobulla's depot. A big box of gold doubloons would be nice, but based on the sender it looked like a stock mix up. Tobulla was hours away and he wasn't going to fix someone else's error today. Instead, he took out his address book and flipped through it.

"Lloyd, Lloyd, where are you?" he muttered. Lloyd Dahl, his parents' barrister; a man who claimed to be the son of Patricia Neal and Roald Dahl. When pressed, he was always evasive about his age and claimed that he was an unwanted pregnancy – dropped off at Saint Thomas' Church in New York, about the time Patricia married Roald. She'd wanted to continue focusing on her film career and had to give him up. To hear Lloyd tell it, it wasn't so much a personal tragedy as a noble sacrifice.

Paul dialled the number. It rang out. He dialled again.

A very English voice answered, speaking in clipped tones that reminded him of John Cleese putting it on a bit in Monty Python. "Lloyd Dahl speaking. Lawyer, Barrister, Attorney, Solicitor and so forth."

"Lloyd, it's Paul –"

"Little Paul Rogers! I dare say I've not heard from you in years. How is your father?"

"Ah, dead actually."

"Truly?" the voice seemed baffled.

"For quite a few years now, but Lloyd –"

"Oh, I am sorry, well, right you are. Sorry to have troubled you. Toodles." He hung up.

"Lloyd, you dope." Paul dialled again.

"Lloyd Dahl speaking, how can I help? Though I must say I am rather busy – I have just now had a crank call and lost my train of thought."

"I, Lloyd, for Pete's sake, it's Paul *Fischer* here."

"Oh, Paul, my mistake. I thought you were a different Paul."

"Indeed. I need some help, Lloyd. Dennis Maddocks is going to sue me for assaulting him."

"Ah." His tone became concerned. "And did you assault him?"

"With vigour, Lloyd."

"Very well. We have got our work cut out for us then. Why not come and see me this afternoon. Four pm?"

"Great, thanks, Lloyd. See you then."

Chapter 5

Before Paul could close up shop early and head for Lloyd's office, Dr Alan Anderson burst inside. What hair remained on his head was a little wild and he'd unbuttoned his double-breasted suit, as though he'd been running. His glasses had slipped down his nose and he wore his 'lecture-face,' it looked as though he was about to spit it out with all the force of a jet engine.

"Paul, you haven't even contacted my office to make time for an appointment, which is rude and obnoxious. As ever, you give not a moment's thought for anyone else, instead you're –"

"Alan, spare me the histrionics – I have an appointment."

"Do you? Well, I hope it's with that joke of a lawyer of yours, because I have something for you myself. It's the divorce papers – and you should know that Rachel is going to be claiming the house and half the shop."

Paul burst out laughing.

Alan blinked. "What the hell is funny about that?"

"She wants a mortgage and half of nothing does she?" He

kept on before Alan could ask another question. "Why did you bother asking to meet with a letter, anyway, Alan? And couldn't you let the magistrate serve me the papers, had to find a way to bring them yourself? Who've you got over there that's an old friend?"

He flushed. "I'm busy, Paul. I simply thought the office staff could save me time with the letter and I wanted to keep things on a formal footing and then you –" He stopped, shaking his head. "Why in God's name am I explaining myself? Look, I thought that perhaps in person, over lunch maybe, you'd be reasonable and you wouldn't drag it out, for Christ's sake. Furthermore, I'm leaving for America in a couple of days." He patted his breast pockets, withdrawing a yellow envelope. "So I'll need these back ASAP."

Paul took a breath, the fight gone out of him in a rush. Was that what the phone call was about? Was it really her? "Rachel couldn't come herself?"

"She's not ready."

"It's been well over six months, Alan."

His expression didn't change. "She's my daughter. I support her."

Paul accepted the envelope. "I'll read over them. I'm sure I'll sign them too, Alan. I'm not going to make it harder than it is."

Dr Anderson raised both his grey eyebrows. "I thought you'd be...difficult about it."

He smiled. "Don't listen to everything you hear about me, Alan. But I do have to make this appointment."

"Thank you, Paul." He paused. "What did you mean, before, half of nothing?"

He gestured to the empty floor. "Business isn't going so

well and there might not be much of a shop left soon. And now that Dennis Maddocks is going to raise the rent to a price beyond my means, it's looking like I'll be singing for my supper."

Alan opened his mouth and Paul thought he saw something like concern pass over his crinkled face. "I really have to go, Alan. I'll get these back to you tomorrow." He opened the door and ushered the doctor into the street.

*

Paul took a few deep breaths before getting out of the car. Rachel. What was she doing? He locked up and stopped, a hand on the roof. Maybe it didn't matter. The quicker it was over with the better.

Lloyd's practice was jammed between White's Dry Cleaning and a new accountancy firm that boasted the best tax returns in the state. Inside he was met by the scent of paper mixing with a large, vanilla candle that rested on the empty receptionist desk. The office itself was simple, the dominance of its white interior unthreatened by any painting. A chest-height reception desk guarded access to a pair of offices, one of which was closed and had a drawn curtain in its small window.

A ginger cat sauntered across the desk and sat itself on the keyboard of a silent computer. "Mr Dahl? Lloyd?"

The second office door opened and Lloyd Dahl stuck his head out. The old man was frowning and he waved a hand. "Come in, Paul, come in, my receptionist is taking a day off. Apparently she is 'entitled to celebrate a religious holiday of her choice' under the workplace act of such and such." He wore a dark suit with a garish yellow tie and his thick, black-rimmed glasses had an authentic Dave Brubeck look. He smoked a giant cigar that looked to be a novelty item. Or it might have been the handle of a baseball bat.

He joined Lloyd in the office and sat in a comfortable leather chair across from the lawyer, who was regarding him with some interest. Behind Lloyd was a shelf of books and journals which were precisely ordered, in stark contrast to the desk, which had been colonised by stacks of paper, folders and pens. A coffee cup had, it seemed, lost a war to spoons, pencils, cigars and an odd assortment of items that didn't fit an office setting – a single blue knitting needle and a Batman action-figure without its head were especially noteworthy.

"Which holiday?" Paul finally asked.

"She was quite vague about that as I recall. I have no doubt she is trying to cheat me. Perhaps I will dock her pay," he mused, then shook his head. "In any event, tell me about your problem. And how are you otherwise, I haven't seen you since your parents' funeral I suspect – how is Henry treating you? Is he still looking out for you?"

"Yeah, he is – nearly fifteen years after I moved out actually, and he's still keeping an eye on me," he smiled.

"Fifteen years? Truly? My, how time flies."

"It does," Paul agreed. "Lloyd, I'm not sure where to start. My wife Rachel and I have been separated for nearly a year. I've even got an intervention order to go with the separation – and just received divorce papers for you to look at later – and on top of all that, my bookstore is failing."

"Your bookstore?"

"I own Stony Bay Books, you knew that."

"Hmmm. I rarely frequent the streets but it sounds

familiar. The lease was in the will, was it not? The building once housed your mother's boutique?"

"That's it. Well no-one wants to buy books anymore, it seems, so the store isn't going so well. On top of that, I'm going to be charged with assault because I slugged Dennis Maddocks. He owns most of Shell Street."

"Ah, him I know. Shell Street and many others. I must say, Paul, that is an impressive black hole you find yourself edging toward there."

"Edging toward?"

He chuckled. "It cannot be all bad then. You almost made a joke just now."

Paul smiled back. "Sort of. But you're right, some interesting things have been happening of late." Kelly Wilson for one.

"Good. Well, shall we start with your side of the story? No embellishments mind, and make sure it is the truth, you know? I find myself addicted to the stuff. Want it all the time."

Paul took a breath and began to explain, leaving nothing out. There was no point trying to make it seem like he'd acted better than he did. He made a mistake, a satisfying mistake, but a screw-up nonetheless. Halfway through his explanation the cat sauntered in and began to nuzzle Lloyd's leg.

"Iscariot, later," he told the cat. "And you have received no summons?"

"Not yet, but it'll happen, I've no doubt."

"True. But it gives me extra time. And I will need it. Maddocks is a man with deep, angry pockets. He will be able to get a court date sooner than us poor folk." He opened a desk drawer and took out a bottle of scotch, placing it on the table. "Better get some cups from the kitchen, Paul."

*

He woke with a hangover that reduced him to tissue paper. Every movement seemed to tear something; his hobbling was Biblical but he managed to make coffee and slump into an armchair. He stared at the cover of Capote's *Breakfast at Tiffany's* where it sat on his coffee table until he realised he was late opening the shop – then crossed it off the 'list of things to do today.'

The wretched excesses of self-pity seemed more constructive, after some of the things Lloyd had told him to expect. If Maddocks wanted to, and he would, the man would be able to take everything. It wasn't just the assault charges and damages the Grinch would seek, it was what he was going to do to the store, forcing Paul out after an assault conviction seemed a given with Roberts onside, if it wasn't already. Having no source of income, Paul would lose the house, although the word 'income' was being generous. But once he lost the business, he couldn't even sell it, something he'd been considering. Or only just realised he was considering.

And he knew all that, knew it just as he recognised the denial he'd been wallowing in. But maybe denial kept him going. Maybe it would kill him too. "You should be terrified," Lloyd had said.

"But I'm not," he rasped to the silent television. At the very least, if he lost the house he could move in with Henry. Still, he didn't want to leave. Paul placed his empty coffee cup down, using gentle movements only, lest the sound of contact with the coaster split his skull open and empty the wriggling mess of underachieving thoughts onto the carpet.

Movement flashed in the garden.

A bird with bright blue plumage alighted on the branches of the gum that provided shade for his tool shed. He leant forward, muttering a curse on Lloyd's scotch as he inched closer. Surely it was the same bird from yesterday, the one that found his wedding ring? And turned up to chirp at him in the car park? Moving its head in slow circles, it hesitated a moment before pecking at the tree. Again, as before, its movements had a very deliberate look to them. The bird continued to do this for some time, a peck here, a peck there, its head rearing back to occasionally examine the trunk. He never saw it strike the tree all that hard. Was it after food?

The phone rang and he hauled himself up to answer it. "Hello?"

"Paul, it's Teddy. Teddy Pendergast from Pendergast Fishing Supplies."

"Teddy, I know who you are."

"Yes, well, yes, of course you do."

"Teddy? I'm pretty hung over..."

"Sorry, Paul – I'll get to it. Some of the Shell Street Seven are planning on having a big sale, you know, a big one, kind of like bigger than Stony Bay has ever seen. Include a bit of a fair, close off both ends of Shell Street and have discounts and promotions and the like. What do you think?"

The Shell Street Seven? It sounded like a classic Western. Was the man forming a retailers posse? Paul could think of a few things to do with a rifle though. "It sounds good, Teddy – if I say 'yes' can I put the phone down?"

"Sure thing, Paul. I'll be around later tonight with some

more details."

"Make it tomorrow at the store," he said.

"Er, all right, thanks Paul."

Paul tossed the phone onto the couch and showered before forcing down some cereal. Something greasy would have been better, but he ate most of the meal before scraping the last few spoonfuls into the sink. He reached for the phone, thinking to call Toshiro, whose Japanese edition of *Tintin in Tibet* had arrived earlier, when the doorbell rang.

"Mr Paul Fischer?"

Two police officers stood on his front step, faces closed, bearing and short hair similar. They had the look of people who were not related but whose profession had moulded them into something of a stereotype. "Yes. Is this about Maddocks? I didn't think he'd wait this long to file his complaint."

"It is, sir. I'm Sergeant Leonard and this is Constable Stevens." He gestured to his right. "Seeing as you seem like an agreeable guy, why don't you tell us what happened in the car park behind Stony Bay Real Estate on Monday afternoon?"

"Okay. After rejecting a plea to save my store, and that of other business holders here, I confronted him. He refused to reconsider and began to verbally abuse me. I lost my temper and assaulted him."

"So you don't deny that you struck him?" Leonard said.

"Not at all."

Stevens raised an eyebrow, as if such honesty were unexpected. "Would you accompany us to the station for further questioning?"

"Am I being arrested?"

The men exchanged glances before Leonard gestured to a sleek car on the road. "No, Mr Fischer, but we'd appreciate your cooperation."

*

At the police station he was processed with impressive efficiency by a happy clerk, then led to a plain interrogation room where he answered the officer's questions in some detail. Sergeant Leonard spoke while Stevens ran the recorder. Paul was honest and the whole interview took less than ten minutes, before he was rushed to another desk. Here he was formally charged and given a summons from the Magistrate's Court, after which he headed home, released 'on his own undertaking.'

A court date loomed over him now. December third. Over a month away yet, but it was there, like a pirate flag on the horizon. He left the house with Tintin in hand, meaning to visit Toshiro, and opting to walk. There was a slim chance the exercise would clear his head but he'd welcome advice just as much. Or even someone who could listen. And few were better listeners than Toshiro. The footpaths became less busy the further from the CBD he moved, having only to contend with old, white dog-crap, a couple of skateboarders and a young family with a pram that was a fully equipped Batmobile with a stripped down body.

Birds were subdued but the traffic snarled at him as it passed. Somehow, he'd almost expected to see the blue bird again. Taking deep breaths, he enjoyed the scents of green life on the air and the sunshine, until a passing diesel engine curled his nose. He cut across a hyper-neon playground to a quieter street. The houses he passed were less impressive than those on Mayfield Drive, but still nice enough. Lawns were mostly tidy, not too many toys left out overnight and no depressing domestics to offset the slamming of doors.

That came some time later, when he crossed the train tracks, courtesy of a stone bridge, the oldest structure in town. He found himself skirting 'Middling Row' which was once named for its location, as a row of ex-commission houses that followed the train tracks through the centre or 'middle' of town.

Toshiro's place was just far enough from the Row to be considered a nicer area of Stony Bay but not upmarket enough for the snobs Rachel had surrounded him with in Mayfield Drive. The house itself was a larger home, built before developers got their hands on every second property and jammed two or three units in the place of one family home. Its low fence was more a formality than a barrier and a stone-paved path led to a welcome mat covered in cat fur.

He knocked and was met at the door by the Iso's daughter, Mei. She had the slimmer face of her mother and her father's steady gaze, but seemed more cheerful than Toshiro, no doubt because, unlike her father, she smiled often.

"Paul, come in." She opened the door wide. "Dad's out back."

"Thanks, Mei. Home from uni?"

"Just for a little while, I've finished my last exam but I'll be heading back to the city soon." She led him through the lounge with its ancestral images and imported folding screens, to the ultra practical kitchen. Etsuko was nowhere to be seen but a large pot rested on her trusty Westinghouse stove, to which Mei went to work, dropping chopped vegetables within.

It smelt fantastic and his stomach rumbled as he passed through the kitchen.

"Patience, Paul," Mei laughed.

He grinned as he stepped outside, manoeuvring over string tied between the setting posts.

"Paul, come, sit," Toshiro said from one of the stools he had set up on the grass. His face was as lined as ever, hair just as grey, but his shoulders were loose and his eyes bright. It was because Mei was home.

"Thanks, Toshiro, I appreciate –" He was cut off by his mobile phone.

Kelly.

"Are you going to answer it?"

He hesitated, finger hovering. He wanted to see her again but right now he needed to deal with what he'd done. Properly. He switched the phone back to silent and put it away. "No, later. I'll talk to her later."

"Her? Is Rachel finally speaking to you again?"

"Rachel...I have no idea what's going on with her. This is someone else."

"Ah. Good," he said.

"Let me try again. Thank you, Toshiro, I appreciate this."

He waved a hand. "I'm happy to listen. It's about your run-in with the Grinch, is it not? The town is talking."

"Wonderful," he said. "Just what I need. But I have something for you first." Paul handed Toshiro the book, and the older man unwrapped the brown paper bag carefully, drawing out the familiar white cover with its unfamiliar Japanese characters. He smiled. "Paul, thank you, this is a treat. You didn't call to say it had arrived."

"I wanted to bring it over."

"That is kind of you." He rested the book across his knees. "All right, tell me now."

Paul almost smiled. The past overlayed with present, and he was a little boy again, Toshiro asking him to explain the principles of JKD as the man stood over him with that same expectant look. "Things are pretty close to falling apart but I'm not afraid like I should be. Or *as* afraid as I should be, maybe. It's like I can't take it in properly."

"And you don't want this protection?"

"Isn't this denial?"

"It could be."

"Well I'm afraid everything will explode if I don't figure this out. It's happened before."

"When?"

"At university. I sort of tore up a newsstand after a couple of big setbacks. They weren't, really, but I thought so at the time. A few bad marks, a breakup, my wallet getting stolen. Crappy things, but they built up and everything came out at once. Not my best moment."

"And what did you do then?"

"Apologised and got on with things."

"And this time?"

"I called Dad's lawyer."

"Good thinking." He gave a nod. "Thomas would approve of that at least."

Paul looked away. "Do you think he'd be disappointed in me, Toshiro?"

"No. He would have wanted you to stand up for others like you did. Whenever he talked about you Paul, even when you were a boy, I could see his pride. But you know he wouldn't want you to bring harm to yourself."

"I do."

"Just remember Paul, you need outlets for all that emotion. You are under a lot of stress now."

"Outlets?"

"Jeet Kune Do is one. Soccer was another. Your wife was yet another. You said yourself – you haven't exploded like that in years, and that was because you had other people and activities to take frustrations out on. Even if it didn't seem like it was so. You take away the outlet, you get an explosion. It's simple."

"So, you think I'll deal with things better if I have an outlet?"

"Hard to say, but I'd hope so."

"What if I have a breakdown instead?"

"Get back up."

"Great advice."

"You are most welcome."

*

On his way back to Mayfield Drive, Paul walked with eyes semi-glazed. He could see where he was going, but his attention was not on the footpath. Toshiro thought he needed an outlet. Should he take up soccer again? He probably wasn't fit enough. Increase his training in JKD? Possibly. More study? Night class? He wouldn't be able to afford that soon; everything he had would have to go to Lloyd, and half of whatever was left would to go to Rachel. And *then* if anything remained, Maddocks would have all of that.

Surfing was free and Stony Bay had clean, spacious beaches with decent lifeguards and pretty good weather; it even had a wonderful shortage of blue-ringed octopus. One of his first dates with Rachel had been at Stony Bay's over-populated surf beach; ice cream and a walk. Hardly inventive, but it was memorable. It'd been thirty-eight degrees. She'd had to use one hand to hold her skirt down, tanned skin drawing his eyes constantly. He'd ordered liquorice and she had peppermint.

His mobile growled at him from his pocket. Set to vibrate, it was as if the ring tone was muttering and grumbling about being silenced. Hopefully it was Kelly again. He could apologise for missing her call earlier and maybe see her tonight.

'Jon Levitan' appeared on the caller ID.

"Hmmm, what now?" He sighed before answering the phone. "Jon, what's going on?"

"Not much, old buddy. I thought I'd give you a while to cool off."

"You have exquisite manners, Jon."

"Yeah, I know. So I've been thinking, you might want to hear about –"

"Not really. If it's against the law, then no."

Silence. Jon's heavy sigh came through the speaker. "It'd be worth a few grand to you personally, Paul. Maybe more. You telling me you couldn't use that?"

"I could use it."

"Then hear me out."

His footsteps on the gravel filled the space of words. Finally he caved. "Tomorrow, Jon. Come to the shop."

"That a boy," he said.

"I don't like it."

"You don't have to, Paul. Just see what you think when

you hear everything."

"I'm not promising anything."

"All right, keep your shirt on."

"It is on. See you tomorrow. After lunch," he added.

"Right."

"See you then." He owed Jon. At the very least, he would listen.

Chapter 6

It was nearing dark when he got home, the pin oaks crowding close, their leaves filtering the street lights. Families were doubtless sitting down to share their meals in the surrounding homes, a yellow glow creeping under curtains and through the frosted glass that shielded their entryways. His own house was dark and empty, but a small figure waited on his doorstep.

Alessandra shot to her feet when she saw him, calling his name in her accented voice. Her face was pale and her eyes ringed with fatigue, a stray leaf caught in her hair. If it were possible, she looked as though she'd lost weight. Where had she been? There was no way, if she had a home, that she was being looked after there. And who knew what, if anything, she'd been eating? She looked to have been sleeping outdoors. Maybe he could try offering her a hot meal, then contact the police. Or even Mrs Greenhorne.

"Alessandra, are you all right? Come inside." He unlocked the door. Once he had her settled, coffee in hand, he found the phone where he'd dumped it on the couch. "I have to call the police," he said.

She gave him a blank look, putting her cup down.

He held up the phone. "*Polizia*, I have to call them to tell them you're all right."

"*Per favore.*"

"They will want to know –"

"Please." She grabbed his arm, eyes wide. He put the phone down and she relaxed, returning to her cup and humming to herself. She looked happy simply to be indoors. Maybe the call could wait until she finished her drink. Paul sat across from her and sipped his own coffee. Alessandra was small enough that her jacket looked too big for her, even though the rips and fraying suggested she'd had it for some time. Her bag rested nearby; it rarely seemed to leave her side. If she did live on the streets, or if she was a runaway, he should find out. Maybe take her to visit the Battisti family and see if they could help her.

That only left the drink to get through – if she even stayed.

And yet – was he making a mistake by inviting her in? He needed to call the police. It was the smart thing to do. It would look more than odd if he just took her in without mentioning the fact to anyone, it would look downright creepy. He was at least twice her age and she couldn't speak English, how would her parents or the police interpret that?

Or Alessandra for that matter.

He'd feed her first. She'd jumped at the sight of his phone and twice already he'd heard her stomach rumble. Besides, how could he explain the difference between calling the police and calling Mrs Greenhorne to the girl?

"Alessandra, would you like me to cook something?" He took out a pan from a cupboard and she nodded, sitting straighter. He smiled and started on some chicken. After a while, Alessandra left the table to browse one of his many bookshelves, running a finger over the spines and taking out a few to look at the covers. He didn't prepare pasta because he didn't want to disappoint her – she was probably used to better – but made mustard chicken with rice instead. It was hot and filling and Alessandra seemed to enjoy it. He didn't say much during the meal, they didn't exactly share a language, but instead chewed the inside of his lip between mouthfuls. At least she was staying put for a moment, but where had she come from?

"Alessandra, where are you from? Where have you been?"

She responded in Italian, her tone questioning, and he repressed a sigh. "Wait here," he said, noting her expression change. "Ah, *uno...minuti*," he tried. "I'll be back soon."

Leaving her at the kitchen table, he slipped out to his garage, going via the laundry, not sure what Alessandra would think if he went out the front door. In fact, he wasn't sure she'd even be at the table when he got back.

He flicked the light on and began pulling heavy boxes from shelving he'd fixed to the walls. Most were books, those he'd read and placed into cardboard hibernation. There were conspicuous gaps, places where Rachel had stored her old tennis trophies and other keepsakes. Beside his criminally underused whipper snipper was the space where her skis once stood, and an oil-spot pattern on the floor served as a dark reminder of her car, the first car they purchased as a couple, a navy blue Holden.

Gone now, both of them.

His school papers, those his parents had saved, were neatly filed in the boxes, but the boxes themselves were not ordered. By the time he was halfway through the fourth, and after killing more than a few spiders, he found his old high school Italian-English dictionary.

Rushing back to the kitchen, he placed it in front of Alessandra with a grin, part of the expression coming from the fact that she hadn't disappeared. "Now let's see if we can get somewhere."

Flipping through, he spoke slowly, using simple words and trying to get the pronunciation right and forgetting about the tense, asking again, where she was from. "*Di... dove...sei?* Um, hold on...*Quale città?*"

She smiled. "*Napoli.*"

"Ah, Naples, excellent," he said. "Napoli, the best pizza," he added.

She nodded. "*Si, pizza! Il migliore del mondo.*"

"And ah, *dove...dorma?*"

Alessandra frowned and he repeated himself, but she only shrugged.

Paul tried other questions and over the next couple of hours they managed to have a short, if difficult, conversation. He wasn't able to learn anything about where she stayed or why she was in Stony Bay, but her full name was Alessandra DiMare, she was twelve and a half years old and had lived in Naples. She was an only child and claimed her parents were both dead, or one of them was, he wasn't sure. It had taken Alessandra a 'very long time' to arrive in Australia but he couldn't figure out any more circumstances. The biggest difficulty by far, was understanding her responses. The words were too quick, and often he struggled to find them, or exact matches for what he thought he was hearing – even when she wrote it down for him.

They had better luck with her bag, which she opened several times to show him a scuffed CD of her favourite band, which was, surprisingly the UK alternative rock band Skunk Anansie, and her favourite book, *Se una Notte d'inverno un Viaggiatore*, which he recognised as 'If On a Winter's Night a Traveller' by Calvino. Had it not been for the author's name and the word '*notte*' on the cover, he probably wouldn't have got it. A plain notebook was filled with her handwriting, but whether journal entries or poetry, he couldn't tell, even when she read some to him. Inside the bag was also the picture of her mother, slid between a folded map, but she did not look at it for long.

Finally they seemed to reach the end of what they could communicate about and Paul served up two bowls of ice cream and turned the television on. Once she finished he would take her to the Battisti's. Or try the police again. She was probably enjoying being warm.

The news reported its usual barrage of 'scum-of-the-earth' material, before wedging something serious between the closing 'feel good' story. A pleasure ship had sunk off the coast during a storm, though operators and passengers; including members of a jazz band, a local politician and an international or two, had survived by clinging to a pair of inflatable rafts. "Amazing," he murmured. Alessandra glanced at him but he didn't think he could explain. Instead got her a second bowl of ice cream and ducked into his room to return Kelly's call. Her phone went straight to voicemail, so he left a message before once again letting his finger hover over the 'zero' on the keypad, lightly stroking it three times.

It was the right thing to do.

He dialled, spoke to the duty officer, who in turn referred him to Constable Stevens, where he once again left a voicemail. Civic duty done, he returned to the lounge room, a slight frown on his face. How could he explain this to her... "Alessandra?"

She was gone.

*

This time he managed to haul himself out of bed early enough that he would actually make it to the bookstore and open by nine, for the first time this week he supposed. Once again at the window with a coffee cup in hand, he saw the bright blue bird, pecking at the gum with the same measured precision – only it seemed to be hitting harder now. Two days running it had done the same thing. He'd have to check the store for books on birds. A nice picture book, so he could identify the thing first. It might have been a robin or swallow. Paul leaned closer to the glass. It could have been the overcast sky, but the creature looked less vibrant. It wasn't alone. The tool shed, the half-coiled hose and everything Rachel had planted in the garden, so carefully arranged in height and colour, seemed to droop. Hopefully it'd rain.

Once he'd opened the store, placing the New Release Grisham stand beneath the eaves outside and setting a brick to weigh it down, Paul browsed the 'Animals' section. No doubt Alan would be collecting the divorce papers sometime today, seeing as Paul hadn't bothered to open the store yesterday, and despite what he'd organised with Teddy and Jon, it was just as possible that he'd have them all dropping in at the same time. Things tended to happen in threes.

He threw himself into the research, carrying a hefty pile of picture books and even a couple of encyclopaedias to the counter. He switched on the sound system, slipped Bill Evans' *Everybody Digs Bill Evans* into the tray and turned it up louder than usual before opening the first book. It was a nice hardcover with large, glossy images. Gloves probably wouldn't have been a bad idea; it was always hard to sell an expensive book to the kind of fussy customer who generally purchased such items, with fingerprints on every page.

Nothing looked quite like his bird, so he moved on. The next book was better, it had a focus on Australian birds and he found a section on wrens, which looked about the right size.

"The Fairy Wren." He slapped the counter top. There it was. A bird of diminutive stature and vibrant blue feathers, with some black and white. The caption was little more than a scientific name and a location, eastern Victoria – inland. Not a coastal bird. He snapped his fingers as he opened an encyclopaedia. "Come on, habits, habits." Nothing he found explained why the bird would peck his gum tree in such a fashion. Doubtless the internet or Alex at the pet shop would have to save the day, but he kept reading anyway.

"Paul Fischer?"

A voice broke his concentration, competing as it had to, with Bill Evans' piano. A familiar policeman stood at the counter, dressed in the trusty navy-blue. Paul's eyes went to the man's gun, then back to his face.

Paul turned the music down. "Yes?"

"I'm Constable Stevens, perhaps you remember my last visit?"

Paul nodded.

"I understand you've recently seen a runaway girl of about eleven or twelve years old, who goes by the name of Alessandra?" the man asked.

"Yes, it was last night. I left a message."

"Which we received, thank you, Mr Fischer." He took out a pad and pen. "At about what time was this?"

"It was getting dark, sometime after dinner. About eight."

"All right, and then what did you do?"

"I cooked her a meal and tried to figure out what she was doing. I found my old Italian textbooks from high school and I managed to figure out she was from Naples."

The officer gave him a look. "You cooked her dinner before you called, sir?"

"Yes, I didn't want to scare her. Mrs Greenhorne, my neighbour, had a similar experience when she ran off at the sight of a phone. She looked pretty hungry to me."

"All right, what else can you tell me?" Stevens asked, gesturing with his pen. "What was she wearing? Did she look sick? Healthy? Afraid?"

Before he could answer, the bell chimed and a herd of elderly ladies filed into the shop. A few looked up at him as they spread around the store, but many simply flocked to the genre fiction, a few groups pairing off to the cookbooks whose produce-rich covers dominated one end of his centre shelves. The hiss of bus brakes followed and he put it together. Tour group. A much younger man followed them inside, and Paul blinked when he recognised Jon. Irrationally, his heart skipped a beat and he stopped himself from waving his friend away. Jon grinned at him and pretended to be engrossed in the new release section.

"Sir?" The constable prompted him.

"Sorry, yes. She looked tired and hungry. And she was wearing jeans and a jacket that seemed too big for her. It was dark green and frayed at the edges. I'd imagine Mrs Greenhorne already mentioned this, but the girl doesn't speak any English."

Stevens nodded. "She has, yes. All right, that should be all for now. Please call me again if you see her." He handed over a card. "Immediately."

"I will," he said. Did Stevens think he was a paedophile? Or was he just worried? The officer let himself out and Jon sauntered over.

"You're early," Paul said.

"I am. Sorry, something got shifted around at work. What was that about?"

"A runaway girl."

The door chimed again, and Alan Anderson walked in, this time dressed in vest and slacks, a camera slung around his neck. A keen amateur photographer, who actually wasn't bad at all, he was placing a roll of film into a pocket when he paused, appearing surprised by the crowd. He came to the counter and nodded to Jon before shaking his head at Paul. "Closed yesterday, were we?"

"Sorry about that." He handed over the paperwork. "It's all signed, an equal split."

"Thank you, Paul."

He caught Alan's eye before he could slip out. "Rachel?"

One of the little old ladies came to the counter, placing a paperback down. Dan Brown. "Just this one, thank you, young man."

Paul served her, offering a bag. "Thank you, madam."

Alan shook his head. "It's like I said yesterday, Paul. She couldn't."

Paul said nothing, only nodded.

"Well then, goodbye, Paul." Alan made for the door. He was prevented from leaving as a man in a suit stormed in. Martin from Stony Bay Real Estate wore a nasty smile. Paul fancied he could feel the bag of shit being hauled toward the ceiling fan.

"You're out, Fischer – you've got until the end of the month, which is more than you deserve." He slapped down an unstamped letter.

"What?" Paul stiffened. "That's not even twenty days."

"Read your terms," Martin said over his shoulder. Paul shot around the counter but Jon and Alan each caught a shoulder.

"Easy," one of them said.

Paul took a shuddering breath and raised his hands. "I'm all right."

They let him go and he noticed a small queue of curious faces forming at the counter. Moving around, he put on whatever was left of his smile and racked up three hundred dollars worth of sales. Nearly every lady bought at least one book; he even sold one of Tessa Kiros' heavy tomes, which was a pricey little item in itself.

Once they'd filed out again, he found Alan and Jon watching him. "I'm all right," he repeated. Alan didn't seem to believe it. "Honestly, Alan. Have a good time in America. I meant to ask why you're going?"

He puffed himself up, just a little. "It's a teaching position at a Boston Hospital; I'm filling in for a colleague for the rest of the year."

"That sounds great, congratulations," he said. Alan made his goodbyes, leaving Paul with Jon, who walked around the counter to join him, laying a hand on his shoulder. It took Paul back a few years, to the front step of his house, hearing what Rachel's operation was going to cost, and Jon saying nothing, just resting a hand on his shoulder.

"I heard about you slugging Maddocks. What are you going to do?"

"After I kill him, you mean?"

Jon lifted his hand and Paul gave him a long-suffering look. "Come on, I'm joking."

"Sorry, I just…you've been on edge lately. For this past year, ever since…"

"I know." He pressed a few buttons on the till and printed off the day's earnings so far. $312.99. "And what am I going to do? Listen to what you have to say. After that, maybe ring the Residential Tenancy Board people."

"Think you've got a chance?"

"After assaulting my landlord in a car park?"

"Good point."

Paul finished up at the till and sighed. "So, let's hear it, Jon. What have you got in mind?"

Chapter 7

Jon set aside his coffee. "No, it won't be like that. I told you, there aren't any cameras on the outside."

It was nearly closing time, and Paul must have chewed the same words over and over. Keeping an eye on the floor from the entry to the kitchenette, he lowered his voice, despite the shop being empty. "What about the driver's door again?"

"Locked, but just smash the window. Use a towel or something." Jon sighed. "No-one will be around anyway and you know where the spare key is. We've been over this, Paul. Come on – you need the money."

"But you don't."

Had a business deal gone pear-shaped for him? The more Paul thought about it, the more he wondered why Jon wanted to help him in this particularly reckless way. Not that Jon would come clean about a failure. And broadcasting failures wasn't all it was cracked up to be. Paul knew that. Whatever it was, Jon had gotten him out of tight spots before. It was what friends did for each other. They helped out.

But it was never that simple. Jon loved his risks.

Jon shrugged. "True. But like you said, I've never needed the money. I'm too damn successful." He grinned. "Besides, can't I help a friend out? I know you've been up against it for a while now."

"You can, but – shit. Is this the only way?"

Jon frowned, voice changing. Was he actually hurt? "I've told you before; I'd help you out if you ever needed it."

"Sorry I doubted you, Jon, but wouldn't it be easier to lend me the money?"

He snorted. "Absolutely, but what do I get out of that? Another debt I can never call in. This way is better – I can buy the new model. Besides, Laura doesn't think it's safe, no airbags, you know?"

He sighed. "But you love that car, Jon. Are you sure?"

"I'm sure."

Paul toyed with his glass. If he did it, well, it was better than having to ask Jon for money again. His friend was right; Paul wouldn't be able to pay him back. He hadn't finished paying for the last bail-out, and Jon had been blessedly patient. More, this time he wouldn't have to hide it from Rachel. Paul doubted she knew, even now, years later, who'd really paid for her operation. Or the roof. Or the first bail-out for the store. "When?"

"Two nights from now. Laura's going interstate, she's visiting her mum."

"All right. Two nights."

*

He banked the store's takings, made a mental note of

how low his savings had slipped, dealt with some overdue bills and drove to the pizza place where he paid the surprised staff for the pizza he and Kelly never ate. He'd have to call her soon. His behaviour was going beyond 'rude' and straight toward 'arsehole.' And he wanted to see her. A lot. But with so much shit going on, why would she want to spend time with him?

After Jon left, another customer came in and right on her heels was Teddy Prendergast with his plans for the 'Shell Street Spectacular.' Something about street performers, buskers, an emcee and 'neat little stalls' in the nature strip, along with some outrageous figure of up to fifty percent markdowns. Paul simply agreed to it all and bundled him off with the right-sounding promises. It didn't matter now – with the proposed date Teddy had in mind, Stony Bay Books would be closed. Poor Teddy, he was trying so hard.

When Paul finally found a moment, he called Kelly but got her voicemail. It wasn't until he returned from the pizza shop, sitting in his wagon outside Stony Bay Real Estate, that he found her. She was leaving, walking beside her pratt of an employer, Martin. Paul kept out of sight – approaching Kelly might besmirch her name.

Once Martin was in his fancy status symbol with wheels, Paul called Kelly's mobile. She hopped into her own car, a smart but reasonably-sized vehicle, and answered.

"Paul, we finally meet again," she laughed.

"Well, if you turn around we can." He stepped out of his car.

"What?"

He watched her twist in her seat, open her own door and then he was hanging up. As ever, she had her 'professional' hair style going, but now he remembered it falling around bare shoulders. His pulse gave a little leap. "I wondered if you'd like to go out tonight, to dinner?"

"Only if you cook," she smiled, glancing at his car. "So, what were you doing hiding over there? Stalking me already?"

"No, I just didn't want to run into Martin. Knowing how I've felt lately, I'd probably have knocked him flat."

Her smile fell. "I heard. I'm sorry, Paul."

"My fault, but don't worry. I'll figure something out."

She placed a hand on his arm and squeezed. "Meet at your place then? I have to go home first."

"Sounds good." He paused. "How about I start dinner? Are you allergic to anything?"

She got back into her car. "Not that I know of."

Paul sped the whole way home, the lingering guilt from a thousand graphic TAC ads barely slowing him. It wasn't until he nearly hit Mrs Greenhorne walking down his driveway that he snapped out of it.

He jumped out of the car. "Sorry about that."

"Really, Mr Fischer, you should be more careful." She frowned. "Are you well? Your face looks a little flushed."

"No, I'm fine, I'm sorry Mrs Greenhorne."

"Well, no matter. I was just coming over to remind you about tonight, Eddie's expecting you."

"Oh." Heat crept up his neck. He was an idiot. "I'm sorry, I can't, it's just that I have a guest coming tonight. It's last minute. I'm truly sorry." It sounded feeble, even to his ears. Her expression killed any excitement he'd been feeling at the prospect of Kelly's visit.

"Oh my. Eddie will be very disappointed, but I'll tell him."

"Tell him tomorrow, rain or shine."

"I'll take that as a promise, Mr Fischer."

"Ah, before you go, Mrs Greenhorne, I wanted to ask if you've seen Alessandra again?"

"No. Have you?"

"Yes, I managed to cook her dinner last night after she turned up on my doorstep, but she disappeared again," he said, going on to tell her what he'd learnt. He ignored the slight frown that crossed her face until he added, "I think she heard me on the phone when I called the police."

"Well, I will say she looked half-starved. Do contact the police again if you see her."

"I will," he said, and she gave a nod as she left.

It wasn't until he'd started cooking that he heard the doorbell. He put a lid on the pasta sauce and went to the door, heart giving a thump as he turned the handle.

He gaped.

Rachel stood under the porch light, a heavy coat wrapping her small frame. Hints of dark hair peeked from one of his old beanies and her eyes were red-rimmed.

"Paul, can I come in?" Her voice put a familiar shiver in his spine. It was enough to confirm what he'd suspected for days. Rachel had called him at the store that day.

"No – I mean, yes. Rachel, what are you doing here?" He rubbed his neck. "Are you trying to force me into violating the Order or something?"

"Paul..."

"I mean, you haven't returned any of my calls and now you just show up – I didn't think..."

"Just let me in, please."

He stepped aside, following her to the kitchen. Her head turned from the stove to the table, which was set for two.

Wine glasses were empty and the serviettes didn't match anything else on the table, but he'd made an effort.

"Expecting company, Paul?" Her mouth thinned. "Am I interrupting?"

"Yes." It slipped out.

"I'll be brief then." Her tone grew curt. He sighed but let her speak. "I came to say that I'm sorry to hear about what's happening to the store. I don't want to make things harder on you. And..." her expression fell. She was worried, he could see that much. "There's something else..."

"You tried to call me, didn't you?"

A knocking cut her off. Kelly called through the front door, her singsong tone putting quite a spin on words that went beyond suggestive.

"I see," Rachel snapped as she stormed past.

"Rachel, wait." He caught up to her as she flung open the door. Kelly stood sheathed in a sleek evening gown, her smile faltering as Rachel pushed by in her heavy coat, her bearing not unlike an echidna, spikes out. She didn't look back, getting into a Beamer he didn't recognise and slamming the door. The engine revved too hard and the wheels squealed as she left.

"Who was that?" Kelly asked.

"My ex."

"Oh."

"Let's go in." He led her to the kitchen and stirred the pasta sauce, a little faster perhaps than was needed. "I haven't seen her in months. We're about to be divorced, actually."

"Really? You don't look too shaken up." She placed her bag on a chair and checked the sauce, inhaling. "Smells great."

"I guess I'm used to it."

Kelly didn't seem bothered either. "How about I serve?" she said. He nodded, staring through the stovetop. Rachel was more than upset. It wasn't just her eyes or the paleness of her skin, the way she'd leant on one foot while she stared at him.

It was the fact that she'd come to him at all.

Was she in trouble? Why didn't she stay and ask for help? If it was serious she would have stayed. She wouldn't have been scared off by Kelly.

And because she *didn't* stay, it mustn't have been too important.

He frowned. Or maybe Rachel was just looking for comfort in the wrong place, looking to use him again? The last time she'd been happy enough to turn up in tears, ask him to hold her, ask him to make love, then disappear afterward without telling him why she'd been so upset. Well, not again.

"Paul?"

He blinked. "Sorry?"

Kelly stood in the pantry. "I said, where's your salt and pepper?"

"Oh, behind the olive oil I think."

"Found 'em."

Kelly looked good. Her dress clung in all the right places and it was cut above the knee, not too high, but enough. A faint perfume reached him when she slid by and she hummed while she worked. An unfamiliar tune, but it was nice and he didn't want to interrupt. Rachel never sung, but she'd always been able to make him laugh.

A groan nearly escaped. He was comparing them now.

What next? Tallies? Pros and cons? Ridiculous. He didn't even know what was going on with Kelly. It wasn't much more than sex. She'd dealt with Rachel's untimely visit with exceedingly good grace. On top of that, she didn't seem to want to go out in public with him. Once already today, she'd turned down an offer to dine out.

While they ate, he made unconvincing small talk until Kelly rolled her eyes. "Out with it, Paul. You've got something on your mind."

"I do. About a hundred things, actually. It'll be able to bench press twice its weight by this time next week." He took a breath. Rachel was gone. Whatever she'd been playing at, she was gone now. "Would you like to go out to lunch tomorrow?"

She put her fork down. "Paul, there's something I should tell you."

"Okay." He swallowed his mouthful and took a drink. In a way, she was a magician about to perform the great reveal – she had his complete attention. Part of him trembled, the other part he was sure would be numb to further shocks.

"It's about my son, Mikey."

Wrong. Not numb at all. "You have a son?"

"Of course, I thought you knew that? He's the reason I take a half day on Fridays."

"I didn't know, actually. Is his father...not around?"

"No, he left us a couple years ago."

"Sorry to hear that."

"Don't be. It's better this way." She skipped over it with a shrug. "Anyway, Mikey's nearly old enough now that I don't want him exposed to...the adult side of my life, I suppose you could say." She shook her head. "Sex, basically. I don't want him to know about it yet. But we're all flesh and blood, right?"

"Right."

"So relax. I'm not trying to do the whole affair cliché."

"Okay," he smiled.

She held out her glass for a refill and he obliged. "So, what about you and your ex?"

"Well, she wants half of everything. Which is pretty much half of zero. Things weren't looking good before I stuffed everything up anyway. She came to apologise, tonight. I think."

"You think?"

"We've not spoken in six months or so."

"Since the relationship fell apart?"

"No, that was a couple of months earlier."

"Geeze, I hear from Greg every now and then. It's not all that cordial, but we speak."

"You have Mikey."

"We'd still talk."

"I tried. I used to call twice a day at first, then three times a week. Then she had my number blocked. I wrote a few times – none of it made a difference. She had her father come and see me, explain that I was one letter away from getting slapped with an intervention order."

"And what happened?"

"I sent another letter."

Kelly laughed.

He couldn't help but grin. "So, now I have an intervention order, one hundred metres and all that."

Kelly was still smiling but she shook her head. "Paul, you know this doesn't make you sound too crash hot. That she would just cut off contact like that, and the intervention order, you know what I'm saying?"

"I do, and it's not as bad as all that – we disagreed about something very important. One of us wanted kids, one of us didn't."

"Oh. Was it..."

He could tell she wanted to ask more but was holding back, unsure how much to press him. "I hope you're not offended, but I don't think I can really talk about it, hope that's all right?"

"I understand," she said. "For now. But you should talk about it, sooner or later."

His stomach muscles unclenched. "I know." He collected their bowls and stood. "How about dessert then?"

Chapter 8

Paul grunted. He'd made his choice. Two nights had passed and now he was sliding up to Jon's elegant Mustang, its eye-catching red nearly black in the night.

The days had flown like blips on a radar.

He'd tried calling Rachel once – no point, she hadn't answered – and then went shopping. He'd purchased black clothing; boots, gloves and a balaclava, ignoring the look he got from the cashier. He'd even tried to find Alessandra again, but no luck, and suddenly it was time to knock off a car.

Gravel scraped and he slowed.

Cold air scratched his throat, his cartoon-criminal-ensemble keeping him warm, leaving only his eyes exposed. Less than fifteen feet away loomed the side of Jon's house, a Jeep parked beside it, and the Mustang in turn – thankfully not in the garage.

Jon's home was a black shape against the stars above. He was out of town on business, having taken his company car, and according to Jon, Laura was visiting her mother interstate. It was all going very well indeed. Once he'd stolen the car, he'd drive it off Quartz Point, and by the time it hit the bottom the Mustang would be crushed, exploded or both. Even the long walk to Jon's had been almost pleasant. All he had to do now was smash the window, take the spare key from the sun visor and he was off.

He crouched beside the driver's door and tapped on the window. Thick glass. He tapped again and discarded his stone, searching for a larger one. In the poor light the garden was just visible, ringed with slabs of granite and slate. Heaving a piece from the earth, he rested it beside the car and took out a rag, which he jammed in the door rim. Hopefully it'd make some small difference to the sound of breaking glass, though Jon's nearest neighbour was some distance away. One of the benefits of living out of town.

Hefting the rock, Paul let the adrenaline build. It was almost like being a teenager again, up to no good...just with adult jail sentences. But he was committed now, and it wasn't as though he'd be ripping off a needy business. Scamming an insurance company that refused to pay flood victims was no problem. No problem at all.

Lifting the slab over his head, he took aim and hurled it at the window.

Glass exploded.

The sickening squeal of an alarm followed. Paul dove forward to fumble with the door, nearly tearing it from its hinges. "Jon, you stupid bastard." Hauling the stone aside, he ripped the sun visor down and took the spare key. Twice he tried and failed to jam it into the ignition. The alarm shrieked on in the dark and he thumped the dash. "Come on."

A light flicked on at the house and he flinched. In the mirror, a well-built man stood on the veranda. Not Jon. The stranger wore nothing but boxer shorts and his blonde hair was ruffled. A woman's voice cried out and the man waved over his shoulder, peering at the Mustang. He took several steps forward and even through the alarm, Paul heard Laura cry for Blondie to come back into the house.

New light gave Paul what he needed; the engine growled into life, flinging gravel from the wheels as he tore down the driveway. The alarm stopped and he heaved a sigh. "Finally." In the mirror the shape of Jon's wife, clinging to the stranger, began to recede. They'd call the police soon, he'd have to put the foot down.

Paul didn't know what had been the bigger shock – that Laura was cheating or that she'd been home.

*

Quartz Point overlooked Stony Bay and waited around ten minutes out of town. His driving had bordered on reckless; but he managed to keep the Mustang on the tarmac and pull into the lookout bay, backing up to the scrub. With the nose of the car facing the bluff and the distant lights beyond, he stopped to tear off his balaclava and enjoy the cool night air. Sweat trickled down his back too, but he wasn't going to strip off just yet. Time was already against him, with the police no doubt already searching. Any wreckage, or worse, explosion, would lead them to him. But there was no other option. The Mustang needed to be totalled, and he wasn't going to crash it into a tree.

Paul rolled his shoulders. The town was a sprinkling of pin pricks on the shore, like a fallen constellation. Anyone who happened to be looking across the water was about to get a surprise. First, he put the car into park and wrenched the hand brake on, then he opened the door, placing the stone slab on the accelerator. The engine revved and he took a deep breath. No practice run for this stunt, Paul.

He pulled the shift into gear and released the hand brake, giving a shout as the car leapt forward. He dove from the driver's seat, rolling when he hit the ground and twisting onto his elbows.

The steering wheel wobbled but the car held true, smashing through the guard railings and sailing over the edge. A terrific crash rang across the bay like his very own personal signal fire. Running over, he skidded to a halt. The wreckage was impressive; mangled bits of steel in a jagged heap, vaguely sculpture-like. He took off to where he'd concealed his wagon earlier – it'd been a bit of a ride back into town, and he'd had to patch a leak in his front tyre before loading his bike in, but he'd managed well enough.

He pulled out of the parking bay onto the highway and switched his high beams on, banishing the shadows that swallowed the road out of town.

*

Nothing Paul did was designed to draw attention. His veins twitched with adrenaline but he kept his hands steady and stuck to the speed limit the whole way to Whedford, driving by a welcome sign with its Rotary symbol and less memorable logos. Being much smaller than Stony Bay, and a mere blip compared to his destination, Tobulla, there was only one motel, but it had a vacancy and he took it. The room was stuffy and small, though it had all the things promised to weary travellers; bed, toilet, shower and heating. It even came with a window that overlooked the silent highway, illuminated but faintly by the large, fluorescent sign proclaiming the Comfort Inn's Vacancy.

Paul cracked the window and sat on the bed, which promptly dipped in the middle. He wasn't sure he dared touch the pillow just yet, certain it could give a piece of paper a run for its money in the 'flatness' department. Tomorrow he'd drive on to Tobulla's mail-sorting centre, one of the largest in the state, where he could sort out the stock mix-up in person – something he'd been putting off while his life was in a shambles. It was a natural reason to be out of Stony Bay at the time of the 'theft.' So too, was wanting to be at the post office early, that way he could relieve Henry at the store sooner, which was an even better reason to leave for Tobulla early and stay overnight at a halfway point.

Everything was worked out. He had nothing to do now but wait for Jon to get back. Nothing, except decide what to say about Laura. It would shatter Jon. He was a flirt and not the most thoughtful man, but Paul had never seen a happier wedding ceremony. But that was ten years ago. Something was obviously missing for the ever-bubbly Laura. Jon worked too much, and since she'd finished up at Stony Bay Primary she'd burned through a whole list of hobbies, each lasting no more than a month. Who knew what it was? But something had changed.

Just as it changed for him and Rachel.

*

The red-themed Tobulla Post Office, its walls and racks lined with impulse-buy items and flustered staff, was too busy to give him anything other than cursory service, but it was enough. He signed for and walked two boxes of stock through the displays and fidgety queue, dumping them on the back seat of his wagon. The sun beat down on the pavement and bounced back up to warm him. A car horn sounded at a nearby roundabout and the brittle laughter of teenagers cut through the general hum of pedestrians and more mechanical traffic.

From the driver's seat, he dialled Stony Bay Books. A few stray elm leaves fell to the grassy strip that split the street. Flowers turned their bright faces up to the sun, expectant.

"Stony Bay Books, Mel speaking."

"Hi Mel, it's me. How are you and Henry going?"

"Fine. It's pretty quiet, though we did have one customer who bought a couple of books."

"Great news," he said. "I just wanted to let you both know I'm on my way back soon. Might stop for a late breakfast though."

"We're okay – Henry's in the back room, sorting to his heart's content, so take your time."

"Thanks, Mel. Tell him I'll have some of those sour lollies he likes so much."

She laughed. "I will."

"See you later then."

Chucking his phone onto the passenger seat, he froze when a blue fairy wren landed on his bonnet.

It hopped around, tiny feet making little scratching sounds. "Hello," he said. It was the same bird. Had to be. He had no way to prove it other than a feeling, but how many fairy wrens had he seen in the last five or even ten years?

Once again the bird was agitated, twitching its head side

to side as it moved. For a moment it grew still, giving him a long look before taking flight. He leaned out the window, sucking in a breath as it flitted before a rumbling truck and spiralled up to rest on a nearby windowsill. There it pecked the wood twice and looked over at him.

Paul left the car and crossed the street.

The bird perched on the second storey of a newsagent. The building above looked residential, pink curtains and a single flower pot suggesting as much. From beside a grilled footpath bin, he craned his neck. The fairy wren stared down at him, dark eyes bright. Once again, it pecked the sill twice, then hopped inside.

The bird wanted him to follow.

Like a Fellini movie. Or a piece of absurdist fiction – doubly absurd because he was going to follow it. Or try to.

He crossed the shopfront a couple of times, excusing himself as he blocked someone, but found no door leading to a set of stairs, no other entrance. The Newsagent had a 'Walkthrough' sign beneath logos of *The Herald Sun* and *The Age*, maybe there was an entry from the rear?

The newsagent was rather spacious. Books and stationery lurked up the back, while large, colourful calendars assaulted him from his left. They were almost tropical in their raucousness.

"Can I help you, sir?" At the counter opposite, a tall woman with hair-care-commercial shine stood beside a girl holding a mobile phone in one hand and a lollipop in the other. She was texting and didn't look up when he approached the stand, which was burdened with chocolate bars.

"Yes. Actually, I was hoping to visit the occupants of the

upstairs room, and wanted to see if I could walk through. Is there an entrance from the street behind?"

Her eyes narrowed. "He's not taking visitors at present."

"I'm sorry?"

"No visitors, do you understand?"

"I don't want to upset anyone, but I saw a blue fairy wren enter the window –"

Her face went red. "You think that's funny?" She spluttered as she leant over the countertop. "A 'blue fairy wren'? Is that a f..." she glanced at the girl. "A *flipping* joke?"

"No. I'm looking for my bird. It flew into your window," he tried.

She bent to the girl. "Call the police, Ruth."

She strode round the counter, a long finger pointed at Paul. "And you get out of here now, you sick bastard. I told him, no more of his dirty friends – that means you."

He raised his hands and backed away. He didn't need police attention – no thank you. "Hey, I'm sorry. I don't know what you're talking about; I didn't mean to upset anyone. I'm leaving," he promised, stepping outside.

"Don't you come back," she shouted.

Paul jogged to his wagon, ignoring looks he got from passing locals. What the hell was that?

He pulled out of the park and circled the block, tapping the steering wheel at a traffic light before pulling into a gravel service lane that led behind the newsagency. He eased the car down the bumpy road, noting a set of enclosed stairs leading to the second floor of the building.

It wasn't worth it.

With everything that was going on, with every thread thinning on the net that hung it all over his head; the Shop, the Grinch, Jon's car and Rachel, it wasn't worth it.

Exiting the lane, he switched the radio on and headed south toward Stony Bay.

Chapter 9

"Are you actually a real person?"

Lloyd Dahl sent a considerable frown across the desk at Paul. The man wore his usual dark suit but his tie was mustard yellow today. Sunlight came through his window and splashed itself over furniture and occupant alike, catching on his lenses. The office was stuffy, thick with the scent of cigars, but the lawyer didn't seem interested in letting in any air.

"What?"

"Well, it is hard to believe how much trouble you've got yourself into – how much business you bring me. An assault and now divorce *and* eviction? I do have other clients, you know."

Paul ran a hand through his hair; it would need to be cut soon. He could have shocked Lloyd with another infraction – Insurance Fraud would have rounded the list off nicely. "Lloyd, do I have anything here?"

"On the eviction?"

"Any of them, I guess."

"Not with the eviction, I regret to say. Stony Bay Real Estate is well within its rights to evict you. The twenty days is petty but seeing as you assaulted your landlord, I can't see the Tenancy Board cutting you much slack."

"Thought so. I had to check, but." He removed his jacket, glancing around for an air conditioner he could switch on, but found none.

"Well, there may be some room to move with the divorce; you say that the split was due to –"

"I'm not contesting the divorce, Lloyd."

"No?"

"No, it's fine – I don't want to make a mess of it. Just keep me afloat."

Lloyd eventually nodded. "That just leaves the assault then. The good news is that I may be able to make a case for provocation and convince the court that you retaliated under duress, it might make the magistrate go easy on you."

"Thanks, Lloyd. That's something. What do I need to do?"

"We just present the circumstances as they truly were and focus on that. Coupled with your refreshingly frank attitude toward your mistake, we ought to get away with a suspended sentence or simply a good behaviour bond. And there may be a fine, or Maddocks may seek damages of course, but that's for the civil hearing later on."

"What sort of damages?"

"Legal fees, hospital bills and so forth."

"That would clean me out, knowing the lawyers he'll be using."

"Probably, but I will do my best to stop it, lad."

Paul offered a weak smile, taking the man's hand. "All right, let me know when you need me again, Lloyd." He collected his papers as he left, saying goodbye to Lloyd's sullen receptionist on the way out.

He'd closed the shop early so he could get home in time to shower before visiting Eddie Greenhorne, and for later, when he was to have a meal with Jon. His friend wanted to eat out as usual; something Paul was happy to do, considering the circumstances. He strode to his car and soon merged with the after-work rush. Eddie was keen to show off his latest creations. Eddie composed on his computer, using software to simulate real instruments. His songs were usually written over long periods, due to a mixture of his physical disabilities and what Paul suspected was a perfectionist attitude.

Once home, he went directly to the lounge window, nearly pressing his nose against the glass. The back yard was collecting fat drops of rain from a summer shower but he could see enough of the gum for his shoulders to slump a little. No wren.

Looking presentable enough in shirt and slacks, Paul crossed the street where Mrs Greenhorne admitted him with a smile. As was customary, her hair was done up and she wore an evening gown of sorts. Two chairs had been placed before a computer in their spacious living area, an easel with a half-finished water-colour pushed into a corner. The smell of potpourri was strong, and from the kitchen the scent of apple pie baking drifted in. A slew of family pictures hung from the walls. The smaller, black and white portrait of Mr Greenhorne might as well have leapt from the wall – it caught Paul's attention every time. Dressed in his army uniform, the man had a strong jaw and a stern eye but he held a baby in his arms, his big hands sure and an almost-smile on his face; a smile that Eddie had told him was equivalent to a beaming grin from others.

"Sorry about last time, Eddie," he said, taking his seat.

"'S fine, Paul." Eddie rolled his eyes but he was smiling, head tilted to the side. "Just give me a minute, okay?"

"No problem." He turned to Mrs Greenhorne while Eddie reached for the mouse. "Mrs Greenhorne, have you seen Alessandra again?"

"Actually I have. She looked troubled so I gave her some water and a sandwich, poor girl. Not more than twelve. Just what are her parents doing? They should know exactly where she is! When I was her age, if I'd been five minutes late from school, they'd have taken me out into the yard and strapped me senseless, by God."

"Hopefully they're looking for her, though it doesn't seem likely."

"No." She pursed her lips. "You know, I did notice something. I just caught a glimpse mind, and my eyes aren't what they used to be."

"What was it?"

She shook her head. "I'm not even sure now. It sounds silly, like I'd be stirring up trouble."

"Isn't she already in trouble?" Paul kept his voice gentle.

"That's true. Well, it was hot and I think she wanted to cool off. She'd removed her jacket while I was in the kitchen and when I came back, she put it on again."

"All right."

"Quickly, as though she were ashamed. I think I saw bruises on her arms."

Paul straightened. "Are you sure?"

"No, not really, Mr Fischer. As I said, my eyes aren't as

sharp as they once were. It might explain her behaviour, however."

"It could," Paul said, his frown deepening.

"I certainly hope I'm wrong. I couldn't convince her to stay, nor have I seen her since. And I have been watching the street, you see," she explained, her voice entirely reasonable, "as I sometimes do with my morning tea, but the phone never stops. Just this morning it was Grace from the Bowls Club. She's having her roses pulled so she can put a vegetable patch in, you see, and she wanted my opinion on –"

"Mum, I'm ready," Eddie said.

"Oh yes, very good, Edward."

"Mum," he frowned.

"Sorry, dear. Very good, Eddie."

"All right, are you both comfortable? It's called 'Seascape Number Four'." He clicked the play button. "The first three weren't good," he added over the opening bars.

Paul leant back. Mrs Greenhorne, sitting beside him, tapped along to the beat. Eddie's music was complex and quite symphonic, with subtle and dramatic changes in instrumentation and mood. She couldn't always follow the beat, he noticed, but her face beamed with pride and she made a wide variety of small sounds indicating her pleasure. She even ignored Pebbles the poodle when it scratched on the door. He closed his eyes. Eddie's song did evoke the ocean; it had swells and crescendos and calmer parts that suggested a ship enjoying smooth sailing. It lasted over ten minutes he guessed, and slowed to a trickle of echoing piano notes that faded out.

Mrs Greenhorne burst into applause and Paul joined her.

"Eddie, that was one of your best. Easy," he said. "What

was that eerie instrument in the middle there?"

"A Theremin. You wave your hands around it to play it, and it looks a bit like an antenna."

"I don't think I've ever heard of one of those," his mother said. "Is it safe for the ears?"

"Of course, mum. A Russian inventor made it in the '20s. Professor Léon Theremin. He made a bug for soviet spies too."

"Got another song then?" Paul asked.

Eddie nodded. "Let me find it."

After the concert, Paul asked to use the bathroom, having filled up on lemonade during the second song, that one a spacey affair, and soon found himself staring into the basin's plug-hole.

What the hell was he going to tell Jon? His friend was bit of a sleaze; he didn't know any other way to relate to women. Or, more likely, he didn't want to know any other way. Even so, he'd never cheated. But Laura? That was a surprise. She was sweet. It was rare that she had a bad word to say about anyone, and appeared to be the chauvinist husband's dream-wife. She cooked, cleaned and made dove-eyes over just the thought of raising children – and did it all with a good-natured smile.

Was she so lonely that she couldn't talk to her husband, and instead leapt into the arms of another man? Was Jon away that often? Paul didn't like it. For selfish reasons, yes – he was in an awkward position, having to break awful news to a friend. But he'd known the two of them for years, since before he met Rachel. It was hard to accept how bad things had become between them. Jon and Laura were pretty solid, or so he'd always thought. What would it do to Jon? What would Jon do to her?

"Mr Fischer, are you all right?"

Mrs Greenhorne stood in the bathroom doorway, expression caught between concern and annoyance.

"Yes, I'm just a little tired."

"I see. I called several times, and I simply wondered if you were well."

"Just not getting enough sleep I guess," he smiled, drying his hands.

She gave a snort. "Doubtless, with your lady-friend visiting."

"That's part of it," he admitted. "Thank you for the lemonade, Mrs Greenhorne. I have dinner plans, so I might say goodbye to Eddie and be off."

"My pleasure, and thank you for coming. It means a lot to my son." Her eyes were moist.

"I enjoy it."

He said goodbye to Eddie, reminding the man that he wanted a CD of all his songs, and dashed across the street to his car. The rain was heavier now, pelting his head as he opened the door. Not in any danger of being late, he still wanted to collect a small gift for Henry and Mel, so he stopped at a bottle shop on the way to the restaurant – this time it was a reasonably new Italian place, *DiFranco's* – the place he had been going to take Kelly.

DiFranco's was well-lit and had a friendly atmosphere, no doubt aided by the attractive waitresses, jovial owner and his quick-witted wife, whose quips floated from the kitchen and into the dining area. One of the girls led him to a table, one with ample room, unlike many restaurants that crammed an extra five tables in anyway.

"Buona sera, my name is Gina, would you like to order a drink to start?" His waitress smiled at him, and held his gaze before looking away. Was she being coy or shy?

"I'll have a coke, please."

"Okay, one coke." She nodded as she left, giving him yet another smile. She was a bit young to be flirting with him. He almost wished Jon would arrive and distract her. Either his friend was late, or Paul was early. Glancing at his watch did little to confirm it. Jon simply said 'seven-ish at *DiFranco's*'.

Someone waved from another table. He waved back as Anton from the Bakery rose to leave his companions and sit across from him. Anton stuck out his hand and they shook. "Paul, hello, how are you?"

"Things are dicey at the moment, Anton. You've heard about the store? And Maddocks?"

"We have, we all have. At least you tried, eh? No-one blames you; Maddocks is a bastard, everyone knows it. But I am sorry to hear it. What will you do?"

"I'm still trying to figure that out."

"Anything we can do to help, you call me, all right?"

"Actually, Anton – there is something."

"Of course."

"There's a runaway girl that's visited me and Mrs Greenhorne a few times. She's from Italy and neither of us can understand her. I was hoping I could have her visit you, see if you can get something out of her? All I know is that she's from Naples, she's about twelve and she doesn't want us to call anyone for her."

"Napoli? I should be able to help, unless she speaks only dialect, though it'd be unlikely with someone of her age."

"What do you mean?"

"Italy's dialects, Paul. Sometimes they're very different, especially in the southern villages. My family is from the north, near Verona. I can get by down south in the cities, but it might not be as straight forward as you think if she only speaks dialect. And that's if she comes back again. You said she's a runaway?"

"I'm pretty sure."

"Have you told the police about her?"

"Yeah. I even have a card from one Constable Stevens."

Anton shrugged, straining the dress-shirt that didn't quite fit him. "Then you've done all you can I guess. Enjoy your meal, Paul. Try the salami calzone."

"I will, sounds good."

Gina the Friendly Waitress brought his coke as Anton left, and he'd barely tasted it when Jon arrived. He was dressed low-key, which for Jon meant not flash but still in designer labels, simply of a muted colour. It actually made him appear more formal, and thus attracted more attention.

"Sorry I'm late."

"It's okay." Paul took a big drink. If only it were cask-strength whiskey, not coke. His lungs were too small. The weight of what he knew was a horrible massage gone wrong.

Jon lowered his voice. "Everything went according to plan. The cheque is in the mail, so to speak. I'll fix you up a bit at a time, spread it out a little."

"Witnesses?" he whispered, the mood contagious.

"None."

Did Jon hesitate for just a fraction of a second? Had it been a way in? Paul chickened out. "What about the police?"

"I told them the truth, that I was away on business and

when I returned my Mustang had been stolen. They think it was some joy-rider. No reason for 'em to suspect anything else."

"Good." He let himself smile, leaning back in the chair. Despite all the precautions he'd taken, it was a relief to hear that the police weren't looking his way. Not that they'd have reason to, but still... "Thanks, Jon. This *is* going to help. I appreciate what you're doing, the risk you're taking."

"We're taking." He grinned, but it faded. "So, how did everything go?"

There'd been a definite pause that time. "You left the alarm on."

A shrug. "Of course I did. Gotta make it seem real."

"Well you could have told me, Jon. It scared the shit out of me." He took a breath. "And it did something else."

"Oh yeah?" Jon called for the waitress and ordered a drink – bourbon, his friend was doing his best to appear nonchalant. "Something else happen?" Jon's mouth was set and he'd hunched his shoulders a little, as if expecting a blow, but his eyes wavered.

"I don't know how to say it."

His friend made no reply.

"Laura...wasn't interstate. She was home."

"And?"

"And there was a man there. I saw them both. I think she's having an affair."

"Bitch!" Jon slammed a fist on the table. Coke and bourbon mixed. Mopping the mess with napkins, Paul waved away the waitress and the owner, who'd taken several steps in their direction. Jon muttered to himself, but his outburst had passed. In fact, he was calmer than expected.

The burden was gone from Paul's shoulders, and it was all on Jon now – but it seemed the man had been lifting weights in secret. He'd already known, or at least suspected.

"You sent me because you knew."

He grunted. "Part of the reason. I wasn't sure. And I am planning to help you out, Paul – I meant that."

"Thanks, but you didn't have to set me up."

"I'm sorry," he said. "But you know I'll be making it worth your while."

"Yeah." He finished what was left of his drink. "I'm sorry too, Jon. Laura isn't the type, I mean, I didn't think she was. You two are good for each other."

"I thought so."

"You'll work it out."

He shrugged. "Well, you ready to return the favour?" His grin was little more than a baring of teeth.

"Like what?"

"Tell me exactly what he looked like, Paul."

Chapter 10

The two weeks leading to the eviction flashed by. Run off his feet, the fortnight compressed into a kind of montage, into mere shades of things when he looked back. He sold books, he packed books away. He saw Kelly, he didn't see her. He watched movies but he didn't read – not old favourites or anything from a stack of new titles by his bed. He played his Jazz CDs, he played nothing. Sometimes he closed up for lunch and just walked Stony Bay. He met with Lloyd and they talked and planned.

On the revised date of the 'Shell Street Spectacular', he and Henry shared the till, actually moving a few books. On his break he strolled the length of the street, ate from Anton's bakery and watched a young busker who'd come out of the woodwork to stun the crowds with his talent on no less than four instruments. Paul witnessed flute and saxophone renditions of pop hits of the day and even a few standards like 'My Funny Valentine.' He placed a fiver in the case as he passed.

"Hey, thank you," the busker beamed between notes, a

gap in his smile.

Paul had barely taken two steps when he saw Alessandra. She walked alone, her ever-present bag slung over one shoulder. He raced forward but she was swallowed by the crowd before he could call her name. For the rest of his break he'd searched Shell Street and its surrounds, even heading down to the boardwalk where he finally gave up, closing his eyes and breathing in the sea air. When he'd returned to the store, Paul filed another report and went back to work, his mind only half on the job.

The majority of his stock, whatever wasn't being returned to publishers, was being moved to his house, a few boxes per trip, driven by his uncle or even once by Jon. Some of the titles he'd try and unload via eBay, some he might sell to bookstores in neighbouring towns. Maybe the manager of Globe Books in Tobulla would help.

The screech and snap of boxing tape being stretched and torn had its own painful rhythm and he covered up small rectangles of his past with every book packed away. The mix of glue and musty pages stopped his hands more than once.

The Shell Street Spectacular had yielded some cash, admittedly nothing spectacular, but enough to have a little dinner party in honour of those who'd helped him.

Arranged around a trestle-table that once displayed ornate hardcovers was the wreckage of Chinese take-away. Lloyd had the remnants of the lemon-chicken before him; he used his finger to collect the sauce, while across the table Toshiro and Etsuko were finishing off the Mongolian beef and black bean vegetables. Jon sat to his left, a bare elbow resting in a pile of fried rice as he chatted with Lloyd. On Paul's other side, Kelly was attempting to sneak the last of his prawn crackers as she laughed at Toshiro's impressions of Paul's first few Jeet Kune Do lessons. Seated between both Etsuko and Lloyd was the Singapore noodles, which Henry was boxing up for later. Mel was back in the city, and Mrs Greenhorne probably wouldn't have enjoyed herself with the company he'd gathered.

"I've realised something," he said during a lull. Cars passed outside, running their spotlights across the bare shelves. All his promotional posters had been taken down. It left nothing for the soft downlights to illuminate, and instead served to thicken shadows and highlight the empty shelves, the light occasionally casting long shadows whenever someone used the kitchenette.

"I am optimistic," Lloyd whispered, loud enough to be heard across the trestle.

"I've realised I don't want to lose the bookstore."

"Bit late for that, isn't it? Seeing as you're handing the keys to Kelly tomorrow afternoon." Jon was tipsy, but there was no malice in his voice. His eyes were wide, as if the announcement was the last thing he'd expected to hear. To date, as far as Paul knew, he was yet to confront Laura. He'd been tense because of it, with a fuse that burnt down quicker than tissue paper. But tonight he'd been very well behaved. Not at all like the arsehole he could easily become when drunk.

"I agree, it is. But...the last few weeks, I dunno. I've had the store for over six years, Jon. I'm going to miss it." He looked at Toshiro. "I think I've been in denial for a long time, about how I felt, about what I could do with this place."

"You see it now," the older man said.

"I do. I don't want to fail, and I have." He held up a hand

to forestall any objections. "I did, I made the mistakes that led to this point. It was my attitude as much as hitting Maddocks." He shook his head, unable to keep a smile from his face. "Geez, feels like I'm accepting an award."

"We'll make you one later," Kelly said.

"Okay. Well, it means a lot to me, how much you've all helped. It feels good, especially in the face of the trouble I've brought on –"

"Spit it out," Jon grumbled.

"All right," he laughed. "I'm just trying to say, thanks for sticking by me."

"Our pleasure, lad." Henry stood, raising his can of lemonade. "Cheers."

"Cheers," the table chimed. Paul downed the rest of his coke and popped the last prawn cracker into his mouth before Kelly could get it.

"So, what will you do?" Toshiro asked.

"I don't know," he admitted. Just a few piles of books remained on the counter. The scents of dust and paper from the empty shelves mixed with pork, lemon and black bean sauce. Even the cash register had been sold to the pawn shop. Old Benjamin had done quite well out of the closure of Stony Bay Books, but it was better than keeping the stuff in a shed.

"An auspicious response," Lloyd chuckled.

"It'll be something good," he said. "I just have to figure it out first."

*

Two pairs of suitably burly men were walking his shelves out and loading them onto a flatbed tray. They were sweating in the morning sun, swearing amongst themselves but probably having a good time. He kept out of the way, busy with the upright from the back room, opening the lid and tinkering with the keys in between non-committal attempts to wipe it down. He still didn't know what to do with it, beyond keeping it and taking it home. Selling the instrument was out of the question.

In the back room he'd found an old poster from the grand opening, rolled up behind dusty display stands. Rachel had done the lettering and the image; an open book riding a bunch of fireworks. He smiled as he ran a hand over it now, where it rested on the piano. They'd stayed up half the night working on it, discussing tiny details and doing their best not to spill coffee on it.

Things had been good then; everything was new.

People who knew his parents would come in and chat and buy new books, old books, anything. He'd argue with his regulars about who was a better drinker, Hemmingway or Bukowski. Sometimes Rachel would surprise him with lunch, or Henry would ring through a bizarre order just to test him.

Now all that was left was vacuuming.

Once the shelves were out he'd have to finish. Rin from the furniture shop, one of Teddy's 'Shell Street Seven,' had given him a good price for them, but that only made it a little easier.

"Last one then." Dave's chest heaved as he lifted, moving in unison with his partner.

"Thanks," Paul said. "And thank Rin again for me if you can."

"Will do."

"And are you still able to deliver the piano to my place?"

Dave glanced at the black upright. "Forgot about that. It's on wheels isn't it?"

"Yep."

"Good. We can have it there later on, we'll do it last thing."

"Thanks again, Dave."

An unfamiliar man squeezed into the room just after the labourers wheeled the piano out. He wore slacks and a woollen vest, sunglasses perched on his head. He glanced at Paul, taking in his rubber gloves and overalls. "How much longer do you think you'll be?" He motioned to someone outside.

"Coming." A second man, this one dressed in a suit, shouted as he burst into the empty store. "Oh," he said, staring at Paul.

"Don't worry, Sanford, he's nearly finished cleaning up. Aren't you, my good man?" Sunglasses said, then drew Sanford to the wall space between windows. "There, you could put that nice statue from the reception hall right there." He turned to the back. "And if we knock out a wall down there, we could expand the kitchen. Martin said it was small, but all the plumbing's in place."

Paul removed his gloves, tossing them to the floor. "And who the hell are you then?"

Sunglasses frowned. "What?"

He took a few steps forward. "Who. Are. You?"

Sunglasses turned to Sanford, who didn't make a peep, and then back to Paul. "I am William Cocteau. And you are?"

"The occupant. So until I hand the keys in, you can leave."

William Sunglasses Cocteau sniffed. "Surely Martin

Roberts from the Estate Agency explained this to you, that we would be moving in early. We have furniture arriving, so finish up here will you?"

Muscles tightened. "Listen to me, Willie." He stepped closer, enjoying the way Sanford flinched. "Martin explained no such thing. I've got things to do here, and you're going to leave now. The keys will be yours when I hand them in later this afternoon. No sooner."

"You can't make us leave." Cocteau was turning red.

"Is that what you think?"

William fell back from his expression. Paul walked him toward the door.

"But what will we do with our furniture?" he wailed. "You have to let us in, you have to."

"Not my problem."

"But we were told –"

"Ask Martin." He had them outside now, Sanford having slipped out first, his suit jacket snapping with the speed of his passage.

"Our furniture, what will we do? It can't just lie in the street."

"Watch me try and care." Paul slammed the door and went back to cleaning, giving the vacuum's power button a thump. Halfway through, he glanced to where the two men argued on the pavement and had to smile. It was petty, but at least he hadn't slugged the insufferable buffoon. Maybe Toshiro was right, that maturity had something to do with second opportunities to screw up – and not taking them.

By the time Sanford and Cocteau left, no doubt to harass Martin Roberts, Paul had already finished the vacuuming, loaded his cleaning supplies away and ordered a pizza. Not long after it arrived, the rumble of a furniture truck pulled into the street. It took some time, but the driver managed to arrange the truck in such a way that it didn't block traffic completely. Not a local company, the destinations printed on the side were mostly city-based.

Struck by inspiration, Paul pulled the curtains down, grabbed his poster and locked up. He met the removalists as they worked on the back doors to the truck. "Good morning."

"Mornin'. You the owner?" the older man asked.

"For another few hours at least."

He stopped. "Huh?"

"I'm sorry to say this, but I'm not due to hand over the keys until well after lunch, and I've got some stuff to take care of inside. There's not enough room."

"You fuckin' kiddin'?"

"No. Whoever told you morning screwed up. My truck isn't coming until after lunch."

The other shook his head. "We've got three other jobs today. We don't have time for this, buddy. Just open up, we'll find a way."

Paul spread his hands. "I'm really sorry but there's no room, my whole shop's inside."

"This is bullshit," the first guy said.

"Well..." Paul paused, as if thinking about it. If they were as worried as he thought they were about their schedule, he'd be fine. And if they were ultimately more concerned about their city clients, he'd be able to turn Martin's childish harassment against the man. "What if you unload the gear here, on the footpath and I'll keep an eye on it. I'm staying here anyway. Got my pizza to finish for a start," he added, pointing. "That way you won't be late to your other jobs."

"Not enough room."

Paul shrugged, glancing around. "I think if we tried, we could fit it here, even if we have to block the front door, which I'm not using anyway. After lunch I'll call the Agent. It's their mistake anyway, they can deal with it."

"Maybe so but this is my business."

"This isn't your fault," Paul said. "I don't know how long you've got to get to your next job but I reckon it'd fit, and it won't be here long."

They exchanged glances. "You offering to help?"

"Why not?"

"Deal." The older man grinned. "Let's make it snappy then."

It didn't take as long as he expected. Paul mostly took care of the boxes while the removalists did the furniture, and in about an hour they were done, the contents of what looked like your typical café stacked right up against the shop, blocking the door and the front windows. It extended out on the footpath, which, while wide, was partially blocked. People had been forced to move around them during the job, but their complaints fell on deaf ears.

Once the removalists were gone, both of whom slapped him on the back, admitting that the man who'd paid them was a 'right prick for treating us like dirt,' Paul found some seats from a nearby stack, sat down and finished his pizza. It was cold but he didn't care.

"Surprised you took so long," Paul called when he saw Martin Roberts running across the Shell Street nature strip, Cocteau and Sanford close behind. They looked like strawberries and cream, two red faces and one whiter than a bed sheet. Two of the colours detached and began a panicked examination of the furniture.

"What's going on here, Fischer, what is this?" Roberts stood with a hand on his hip, waving an arm.

Paul stood. "Furniture."

"I can see that," he ground out.

"Seems like there was a mix up with the delivery times – you wouldn't know anything about that would you?"

Martin ignored him. "Fine, give me the keys then."

Paul shook his head. "I can't, I left them at home. But I'm sure you've got a set at the office, right?" He started walking away. "Help yourself to some pizza, Martin."

"We're going to screw you in court, Fischer, you know that?"

Paul waved his rolled up poster but didn't turn back. Being petty was better than breaking the man's nose. Just.

Chapter 11

An hour or two later, after switching his phone off and driving across town to help Toshiro oil the decking, he dropped the keys in to Kelly, who smothered her smile in front of Jenny. His arms ached and his back could have been a reworked piece of origami but he managed to stay upright as she took him aside.

"I heard what you did. Martin's still out there trying to calm Cocteau down."

"Good."

"So, how does it feel, giving it up?"

"It's okay. I said goodbye last night."

"Sure?"

"Yeah. I've had time to get used to it, I suppose."

She raised her hand as if to take his arm but stopped. "All right, see you tonight then."

At home he began listing a handful of first editions on his new eBay store – named, imaginatively, Stony Bay Books Online. He'd started work on a new logo too, sketching idly and pausing, pen frozen, when he saw what he'd drawn.

The silhouette of a wren.

He blinked and pushed the paper away. Back to real work. He added sets and rarities next. There was no point bothering with the bulk of his stock, it'd take a year just to do the History section. He'd try specialising in rarer books instead. See what happened.

Paul had several coffees while he worked, keeping an eye on the garden for the wren, which he didn't see, and an ear out for Dave. Later, he'd have to go climb the tree, see what the wren was doing, but the fractured pieces of his business came first.

He'd added a few titles to his simple store, and was listing his business at various sites when Dave arrived with the upright, which Paul had placed in the lounge. He'd already had a drink when Kelly arrived for dinner, offering to cook and effectively manoeuvring him out of the kitchen.

"That smells pretty damn good," he said as she worked. "What is it?"

"Just chicken with chives and garlic, I've added some greens too." She checked on the beans. "So what will you do now? Run everything online?"

"For a while. Tomorrow I'll probably go to Tobulla with whatever stock's left and drop it off at a bookshop there. I spoke to the manager, Freddie, a guy I know, earlier today and he's going to help me out."

"There's no one local?"

"Not anymore."

"Oh, sorry." She moved around the bench to kiss his forehead, one hand holding a wooden spoon. "You'll be fine."

"Well, I have all my suppliers and I can still order through them but..."

"You don't want to sell books anymore?"

"No, it's not that. I want the store back, and the more I take myself down the online road the harder it might be to go back."

"So why are you selling so much stock?"

He hesitated. "Because it doesn't look good, does it?"

"No, but you seem to have an idea." She kept half her attention on the meal and the other half on him. "At dinner last night."

"No ideas, just promising myself I guess."

*

Dawn scratched its way across his eyelids and he hauled himself out of bed with a groan. After Kelly left last night, shaking her head at how often she'd been calling her babysitter and joking that soon she'd have to start splitting the bill with him; he'd spent time on his listings, more out of a sense of duty rather than from any hope or excitement. Too much time as it turned out, judging from his headache.

He showered and grabbed a banana from the bench, first checking the garden for the absent wren, then finished loading Henry's small trailer with books and pulled out of the driveway.

The rising sun filled the street with rich shadows, bolts of gold sliding through the leaves. Joggers were out and about, their faces serious and clothes suitably 'work-out' but not all that dissimilar to the matching tracksuits often worn by the elderly. Traffic was light and he left the sleeping town quickly, heading up the coast and flicking a glance at Quartz Point as he passed. Empty, and the ocean beyond was calm, its waves a bare curling of a lip before they hit the shore.

How much of the Mustang was down there?

He drove on.

While the prospect of Freddie from Globe Books taking a good deal of stock off his hands was something of a relief, how could he really enjoy it?

"Where are you then?" Surely the fairy wren would have appeared again by now, especially as it seemed to be able to find him anywhere. The trip to Tobulla could have waited. He didn't need to rush six hours up the coast to find another bookstore. Others were closer, perhaps not as large, but certainly closer. Two hours south of Stony Bay was one of the only Borders stores in the state to actually survive the REDGroup collapse.

He wanted to know what was above that newsagent.

Why did the wren want him to go there? Who, or what was inside? Most likely he was making a fool of himself, driving six hours to burst uninvited into some poor fool's home. Uninvited being something of an understatement. The woman in the Newsagent was on edge. On a tightrope. But she'd suspected him of already knowing what was upstairs, that's what set her off. He frowned. No, when he mentioned 'a blue bird' she thought it was some offensive joke, that's what really got her going.

He stopped for a late breakfast in a roadside service station, getting a bank balance from an ATM before filling up the wagon. Down to his last few thousand dollars, his own tightrope was thinning. Steel cable was twine. Dental floss was next, no doubt. Jon's insurance money was supposedly about a week away, and whatever Freddie could offer would be a help, but a cold pit grew in his stomach. It wasn't getting better.

With no rent on the shop, he'd reduced his expenses by half. Not all bad. But it left house payments and other living expenses, on top of which his income, already failing, had potentially been reduced to nothing. He had the online store, but who knew how it would fare? And he couldn't keep relying on handouts – scams in Jon's case – from friends. He needed something real. Despite the bravado, he didn't have any ideas, no clever plan. The store was gone for good. He'd fucked it up and was left with a house he didn't own, several hundred kilograms of unsold stock and a slew of legal issues. What he did have was a degree in business management, a crazy bird stalking him and a headache. He could start a new business, but in what? And where would the money come from? Maybe rob a bank? Useless. He was better off committing suicide.

Or committing murder.

He laughed. The last one was tempting. He didn't own a gun, but he'd do it with his hands for Maddocks. Paul overtook a caravan, putting the foot down. They should've been banned from highways already. With no inclination or ability to drive at a speed even approaching the limit, they were menaces, like giant steel snails painted white for visibility. He kept on a bit, the insane blur of trees and farmland suiting his mood.

Sirens flashed in his rear view mirror and he swore. A police cruiser was closing in fast. He braked, hands white on the steering wheel as he eased himself onto the shoulder. How could he be so utterly stupid? The car pulled in behind him and the officer switched the siren off, but left the lights flashing. It was like a beacon to all on the road – look at this idiot everyone, he's been caught speeding. Just as the officer reached his car, the damn caravan trundled by. Salt in a wound. "Idiot, idiot, idiot," he muttered under his breath.

"Sir, do you know why I've stopped you today?" the older man asked, pad in hand.

Paul nodded. He had to be very careful here, not only to suppress the seething flow of rage that was directed at himself, but not to be a fool either. He'd had more than enough police attention lately. "I was speeding."

"Yes you were. About twenty-five kilometres over the limit. Any particular reason for that, sir?"

He rubbed his forehead. Instant loss of licence. "I wasn't paying attention, after I overtook that caravan. I should have slowed down sooner."

The office made a sound of agreement. "And what's in the trailer, sir?"

"Books."

He removed his spectacles. "A lot of them I see."

"My bookstore just closed down and I'm taking some leftover stock to Globe Books in Tobulla."

He nodded. "May I have your licence?"

Paul produced it and listened to the crunching of the man's boots on the gravel. The cars flashed by on the road, one even beeping at him, a jeering cry caught by the wind of their passing. He sat clenching and unclenching his fists, breathing deeply. It was mind boggling, how complete a job he was doing of ruining his life. In the rear view mirror, the officer was still in his car. It seemed to be taking a long time – Paul had received speeding tickets before, two of them in the same month a few years ago, and didn't think it should take so long. Was it about Jon's Mustang? The intervention order? His assault charge? The officer had options at least.

Minutes dragged on. He sweated in the sun and wound the passenger window down. When the policeman finally returned, instead of handing back the licence, he glanced at the trailer.

"Mr Fischer, I'm going to ask you to step out of your vehicle and open some of these boxes, do you understand?"

"I do." Paul did as instructed. What now? He fumbled as he untied the corner of the tarp and took the first box, with Henry's clear handwriting on the top 'Thriller' and unfolded the flaps. The officer looked inside, nodded and gestured for another. This one was marked 'Children's' and once he'd poked around inside for a bit, eyes fixing on the Stony Bay Books stickers, the officer gave a grunt.

"Thank you, Mr Fischer."

The tension in his shoulders eased. "Did you want to check the ones in the car?"

"No need for that." He was silent a moment longer. "Twenty-five kilometres over the speed limit."

"Instant loss of licence."

"For a month at least. And four demerit points. On top of all your other troubles, it's a shame." The officer met his eyes. "I might just be lenient today, in light of everything else, Paul."

Paul blinked. "Do we know each other?"

"No. But I knew your father and I owe him at least this," the officer said, turning to leave. "Just keep an eye on the bloody speed limit, all right?"

"Wait, who are you?"

"Senior Constable Sean Phillips – your dad and I did basic training together."

"You were in the army with Dad?"

"We were. I was smaller, younger and stupider but he looked out for me. We lost touch after I went overseas, and now I run into his son over thirty years later. Odd how random these connections are, aren't they?" he remarked. "Just remember what I said." He went back to his cruiser, Paul still standing beside his car when Senior Constable Sean Phillips drove off with a wave.

He exhaled. Finally some good luck – and he knew what his father would have said. Don't waste it, son.

*

Globe Books towered over the street, dwarfing a nearby chemist and a café whose outdoor setting was filled to capacity. Without the sea breeze to offset the sun's hammer blows, he began to sweat as heat bounced off footpaths spotted with old bubblegum and the odd cigarette butt. Painted blue with a diagonal stripe, the two storey building boasted books, CDs, DVDs and more, the word 'more' having an exclamation point that threatened the 'S' on 'Globe Books.'

The air-conditioning beyond the sliding doors nearly knocked him down but he paused to enjoy it. Having walked round from the back, sweat already trailed down his neck.

Books were arranged on the ground floor under genre-headings in a mixture of spines and eye-catching covers – or they would be eye-catching if they weren't all designed to be so. It was something the publishing companies had to fight, the clutter their own products contributed to. If the author was big enough, their new releases came with display stands or even instructions on how they had to be displayed. But too often they were all lost in the clutter.

Glittering rows of CD and DVD racks winked at him from the first floor of the 'bookshop' but he ignored them, going straight to the rear of the ground floor. He was half a dozen steps from the door to Freddie's office when a voice stopped him.

"Can I help you, sir?" A young woman with a uni-student look beamed at him with the forced cheer of retail.

"I'm okay, just here to see Freddie."

"Oh, okay then. I think he's on the phone but he's in at least," she said, her smile becoming genuine. He thanked her and slipped into Freddie's office, where the man was just putting the phone down. A wall-sized painting of a desertscape hung behind him and on his wide desk rested framed photos of his family. "Paul, take a seat." He waved to the chair opposite, squeezing a handshake in. "Good to see you again."

"You too, Freddie."

"You find the back entrance okay?" His round face had not changed. The man was clean shaven and not a hair was out of place on his head, even his eyebrows had an almost-sculpted look. 'Neat' was a lesser descriptor for Freddie when it came to personal appearance. They'd met several times at Bookseller's conferences, when he used to go, and Freddie had been helpful when Paul first set up Stony Bay Books. Hopefully he could be as helpful now, at the end of the store's life.

"Yeah, it was a bitch to get the trailer in though – and no-one answered when I rang the bell," he laughed.

"Sorry. I must have been on the phone, but I know what you mean about that alley." Freddie gestured to a mug of coffee but Paul shook his head and the neat man continued, his expression becoming sombre. "Sorry again to hear about your store, Paul."

"Thanks, Freddie. How are things going here?"

"If we weren't diversifying, it'd be tough. But we're doing okay. I had to cut shifts back a few months ago, but things might be on the upswing again. Slowly, anyway."

"Good to hear. So, think you can help me?"

"Of course, but you know I can't offer you much. I can't return any of the stock you give me to the supplier and –"

He raised a hand, smiling. "It's okay, Freddie, I know how it works, you know? Fellow bookseller here. Whatever you can manage is fine."

Freddie chuckled. "Of course you do. All right, let's have a look and I'll figure out an estimate, then have a cheque for you by the end of the week, if you're lucky."

"Sounds good."

While they picked through the boxes Paul asked about the newsagent.

"Don't really have that much to do with them," Freddie replied, a pair of historical fiction titles in his hand. "The woman, Sandra, is a little grumpy but they don't have a wide selection of titles. I doubt they'd take much from you."

"I thought I might check. They might discount some of the titles you don't take."

"Maybe."

"But maybe not," Paul said. "You said she was grumpy?"

"Yeah, she always seems tense. And made right up – nothing out of place, you know? Goes a bit overboard I think." He placed one of the titles back and kept the other. "Home-schools her kid, so that might be why she's so out of sorts all the time."

Paul held back a smile at the description the fussy man gave of Sandra and nodded. "I'll chance it while I'm here, it's a long drive after all." He left it there, and shifted the conversation back to the task at hand.

Sorting the titles took a couple of hours, and by the end Freddie had made him a reasonable offer of a thousand dollars even, which Paul shook on. Considering the volume and condition of the books, he probably deserved a little more. A fraction of their worth of course, but it was better than nothing and Freddie was taking on something of a risk himself. "I'll send off the cheque, Paul. I've got your home address, don't I?"

"On the paperwork. Thanks again, Fred."

"Glad to help," he said as he left.

Paul loaded the few remaining boxes into his wagon and snibbed the storeroom door on his way out. The sun still pummelled the earth in the alley but a slight breeze had picked up. It chilled the sweat on his face, hands and neck. He wound the windows down to let some air circulate. When he did hop into the car, the rumbling of his stomach led him first to a spot near a park with flowerbeds and bench seats, where he could fit both wagon and trailer, and then to a salad roll from a deli.

Once he finished eating, he strolled the streets until he reached the newsagent. From the second-storey window the fairy wren looked down at him, blue feathers bright against the dark building.

"Time to get the news," he breathed.

Chapter 12

Trying not to sneak, Paul walked the uneven service lane that led behind the newsagent, shaded from the sun by rows of buildings. Their backs were weatherworn; lacking paint and signs, occasional windows boarded up or left to gape. From their shadows he imagined eyes tracking him.

Ridiculous.

Having already checked that Pantene Sandra was busy with customers, and little Ruth was occupied with her phone, the odds were in his favour but he still wanted to be quick. Neither saw him; he'd chosen his moment, ducking in and out during the lunchtime rush, and was now working to slow his breathing as he reached the steps leading to his destination. A single door with no window and a heavy lock waited for him. He tried the handle but it held.

And that was it.

"Sorry birdie, maybe I'm not going in after all." He crouched to search for a hidden key on the bare landing, almost as an afterthought. Nothing. He rose with a shrug but stopped at a scratching. It came from the door. His eyes widened when a tarnished key slid through the gap between floor and door.

"Hello?"

Only the distant hum of traffic. He scooped up the key and fitted it to the lock, hesitating. The stair was empty and none of the buildings opposite had shouting, pointing people in their windows. All was calm and still. Go now or go home, Paul.

He turned the key and stepped into a dim hallway, closing the door behind him. Empty. He shivered in the silence. Had the wren given him the key? A closed door let light creep in around the frame at the opposite end of a corridor. He inched forward. A thick runner muffled his steps and the closer he came, passing other, closed doors, the more he imagined the feel of cold handcuffs slipping over his wrists, the words 'breaking and entering' echoing in his head.

He paused, one moist palm coming to rest on the handle. The sound of a television, turned low, exhaled through the wood. On the other side would be something important. Or nothing important. Maybe the bird wasn't there. Maybe it was simply crazy. As crazy as he was for following it. "In we go."

Open windows let light and air into a room piled high with all manner of mess. Dust motes played. The place put Llyod's desk to shame – this was the clutter of years. True hoarding.

An actual trail, like a forest path, led to strategic positions in the large living area; the window, the murmuring television, another doorway and the entrance to a kitchen. His view of the whole room was blocked by a bookcase and the jumble that had formed before it. Towers lined the path, some were chest high and others much lower. A few were even taller and all had to be navigated through. Mostly newspapers and books, or magazines and pamphlets. There were also war camps of LPs and 45s, some naked, some with sleeves. Empty bottles formed odd palisades, armchairs were invisible beneath piles of clothing, not unlike multi-hued, soft fungus, and more than a few of the boxes had become shelves for statuary or appliances that sat there, mute as decommissioned machinery. There was even a toy train set; one of its carriages hung from the top of a cabinet. The engine and other carriages rested atop and all were covered in a layer of dust that cloaked the original colour.

Several steps in brought him level with a bookcase. It stood draped with scarves and scraps of paper that could have once been posters, and wind chimes with socks and rags stuffed between their bells. Twisting like a slow-motion belly dancer, he moved deeper into the apartment, narrowly avoiding an ironing board set like one of the spinning blade traps from *Indiana Jones and the Last Crusade*.

At last a lounge-suite came into view, hulking across from the half-buried television, and, more importantly, the occupant of that couch.

A dangerously overweight man sat wearing a bright blue bird costume.

Paul froze. Details swam. The man must have weighed over two hundred kilos. His face was unshaven and his hair lacklustre, the glazed eyes barely moved and collection of drool dripped from chin to chest, right down to the couch itself. Cream coloured and relatively free of clutter, it had a vague flower-pattern. A half-eaten packet of chips sat beside a remote and a glass of water rested on a small table.

This was what the wren, wherever it was, wanted to show him?

"Hello?" he ventured.

The bird man did not react. The rise and fall of his chest remained constant but he didn't twitch and his eyes didn't track Paul as he came closer. "Hey, can you hear me?" Still nothing. Paul waved his hands in front of the man's face, blocking the television. The slightest frown broke the big guy's forehead, but nothing else.

"God, this is not good." He checked the kitchen – an immaculate series of surfaces and floor space. It was white, powerfully white. The tiles were like mirrors and the oven sparkled. An electric mixer caught light where it came through the window with the flower pot, and a spotless sink had a single tea cup within. The fridge door was unadorned save for a shopping list written in a precise script. It was held up by a strawberry-shaped magnet, looking like a bloody red spot in the bleach-white room.

And still no fairy wren.

Why had it led him here of all places? Did the wren and the man know one another? Maybe the wren thought he could help the guy? If so, the bird was just as crazy as Paul was for breaking inside in the first place. He couldn't think of anyone worse for the job. And he'd made a mistake. It was time to leave, before someone came to check on the man.

The door to the apartment opened and he froze. A humming preceded Ruth, whose skipping feet slowed when she reached the entrance to the mini maze. Her hair wove through the columns and he shrank back against the fridge.

"Hello, Brian." Her small voice was bright. "I hope

you're feeling all right today, Mum says you should be." She disappeared into one of the rooms beyond the couch, and shouted back to Brian. "On the weekend she says you'll have a visitor, won't that be nice?"

Paul hopped onto one of the benches, hiding himself again, knowing that when Ruth left her room, she would see him if he stayed put. From his new vantage point, he saw her clamber onto the couch and kiss Brian. He met the man's eyes, but had no idea if he registered in their glaze.

"Bye for now," she said as she wove out of the lounge, closing the front door with a click. Paul waited a moment and slid down; wiping at the scuff marks his shoes left before passing Brian and checking the window. Still no wren – why had it brought him here? He should leave, he knew, but instead he stuck his head into Ruth's room, and found it only slightly less orderly than the kitchen. The next room was obviously Sandra's. He hesitated. The utter violation of what he was doing was impossible to deny any longer. Especially with Brian the bird man sitting mute and spaced out on the couch. Somehow, that made it much worse.

But the mysterious fairy wren wanted him here for a reason.

An open book was the only object out of order in yet another clean room. No marks on the carpet, bed made as if it had been re-starched and the walk-in dresser closed, with ornamental lavender tassels hung across its handles.

He took the book and whispered the last entry, dated some weeks ago. "We have not been able to remove the ridiculous suit he made but in any event, it's one of the only things that fits him. God help me, it's too much. Brian's most recent medication is the worst. And the best. It totally removes his personality and his will or ability to do anything. I am afraid to admit that I prefer this to what he was before." Paul placed the journal back on the bedside table, hands shaking. That was enough.

In the next room, he went directly to Brian. "I don't know if you understand me, but I promise I will never come back here," he said, trying to force his words through the man's stupor with the strength of his promise. "I hope you heard that somehow."

Picking his way back toward the door, stomach still unsettled, Paul flinched when a voice gurgled behind him. "Rachel."

The fairy wren sat on Brian's shoulder.

It was very still, but did not break eye contact with him. Brian had straightened his bulk somewhat, and his empty face now turned to Paul. "Rachel," he repeated. Paul's jaw went slack. The bird's beak moved but no sound came out, instead it was the semi-comatose man who spoke.

"Rachel." This time the voice had some urgency to it.

"I..." he trailed off.

The man trembled, head lolling to one side and his eyes rolling. "Rachel," he repeated before falling silent. The fairy wren twitched a glance at Paul, hopped to the window and disappeared.

Paul knocked over several bottles in his haste to check the man. Brian was breathing, but that was all. "Brian, can you hear me? Has something happened to Rachel?" He struggled to keep from shouting, glaring at the window. "Damn you, come back."

The bird didn't reappear and he drew a deep breath, taking Brian's head in his hands. The man's skin was slick with old sweat. "Brian, can you hear me at all?"

Nothing.

He let the man's head roll to the side and stood. There was nothing he could do without revealing himself, and so Paul straightened the bottles and left, casting a final glance over his shoulder. Brian was still.

*

Night had fallen but it was hardly inappropriate to visit Rachel, not much after seven actually – appropriate, of course, if he was willing to pretend the intervention order wasn't still in place. But if she could violate it of her own accord, not a month after putting it in place, and then again months after that, Paul would too. He'd been willing to do it before, what did it matter now?

He'd driven on to Grady's place once leaving Tobulla, not bothering to go home first. He had to know.

After he'd stopped trembling and running the scene in Brian's apartment over in his mind, everything was clear. Check on Rachel. To hell with the intervention order, things had gone so far beyond it now. Every step back to his car, he half expected a voice to shout after him, a heavy hand to come crashing down on his shoulder. But neither happened and he knew he'd gotten away with it, 'it' being, somehow, one of the worst things he'd ever done. He had hours behind the wheel to come to terms with what he'd done. And seen. Or heard. The fairy wren had been speaking to him, *through* Brian. It was the strangest, most unbelievable thing it had done – but not the only strange thing.

He would be a stone-cold fool to ignore it.

How long had it been trying to get him to go to that

house? Somehow the wren knew he was going to be in Tobulla. But nothing explained the connection to Brian. Was he the only conduit available? Was the poor man so drugged out of his mind that he could be used by the wren?

It went beyond freakish coincidence. That Brian's toasted mind could be calling for another person named Rachel, or even the possibility that he knew Rachel herself, somehow was just...Paul didn't know.

"It wasn't a coincidence," he told himself for the hundredth time. 'Ruth' and 'Sandra' were the names of Brian's family. And the bird had been so still, so intent. Every move purposeful.

Grady 'the Mayor's son' Dolan wasn't hard to track down. A phone book in Paul's car gave up the address. It was hard to tell as the street lights were few and far between, but the man's house had to be expansive. There was no gate, though the driveway was long. Pulling up in the miniature gravel roundabout, Paul made sure the lights were on in the large house before he cut the engine. An ornate knocker, worked into the shape of a rose, got the required attention. A blond man in slacks and a plain blue business shirt answered the door, a glass of wine in one hand.

"Yes, who is it?" He looked Paul up and down. "Do you know what time it is?"

Paul covered a moment's surprise with a cough. He knew this man. Or rather, he knew Grady from somewhere else, despite never having met the mayor's son before. "I'm sorry, I know it must be dinner time, but I was hoping to speak with Rachel. She's an old school friend, you see."

"Really? Who are you then?"

"Irwin Fletcher," he said, using the name of one of her

favourite movie characters. Maybe Grady had seen him in an old photo of Rachel's, if she'd kept any, but the mayor's son didn't blink when Paul lied. "I'm sorry to show up unannounced, but it was a spur of the moment thing. I didn't even know I was going to be passing through Stony Bay today."

"And how did you get this address, Irwin?"

"Alan's secretary gave it to me," he said, remembering the man was still overseas.

"I see," Grady said, then shrugged as if finally accepting his story. "Well, you can't see her anyway, she's not well."

"Oh, I'm sorry. Is it serious?"

"No." He put a hand on the door. "I'll tell her you dropped by, Irwin."

The door closed and Paul swore, running to his car and driving to the roadside where he took his mobile and dialled Rachel's number.

Voicemail.

"Rachel, it's me. I'm calling to see if you're all right. Something happened and I'm worried about you, can you call me back please?" Would she do it? There was no way to know, and nothing else he could do for now. "What the hell is going on?" He thumped the dash before jamming the car into gear and heading out of town again, this time toward Jon's house.

*

Jon's face nearly slid from the front of his skull. "She's what?" It came out as a hiss. They stood in his study, a large room filled with calendars, plans and artists' renderings of building developments. Two laptops sat at different desks. Resting on one, Laura's by the rainbow of post-it notes arranged around it, was a copy of *The Very Hungry Caterpillar*. A small stereo crowded into shelves, which Jon switched on to cover their voices. Laura was in tonight, watching television between batches of chocolate and hazelnut muffins.

When he'd first arrived, Paul managed to get through a few minutes of small talk with her before letting Jon whisk him away, not a moment too soon. Spending time with the both of them was uncomfortable, but he didn't let it show. He hoped. Now he was watching the man choke the imaginary life out of a stress ball, its comical face distorting. "That prick."

"I know."

He pulled a computer-chair from the desk and pushed it to Paul before taking his own. "So you're sure it was Grady you saw here that night?"

"I am, Jon. Grady Dolan is cheating on Laura with Rachel. Or on Rachel with Laura."

"That piece of shit."

"I agree." Paul shoved his hands into his pockets. They were shaking but giving Grady a thrashing wouldn't solve anything, even if it might make him feel better. Keeping an eye on Jon was probably more important.

His friend stood and paced in his robe. "And you went out there? Just out of the blue to see Rachel and he answered the door?"

"Not quite out of the blue. I'm worried about her." He didn't say what prompted the visit. "She came to see me one night, not too long ago. But she took off when Kelly turned up for dinner. I hadn't seen her for months." He shook his head. "I think she wanted to tell me something."

"Ah-ha."

"And now she's supposedly sick, and her mobile phone is off. It usually rings out – she *never* turns it off. She's addicted to it, Jon."

He nodded. "She used to check it every half hour, used to interrupt our card games."

"I remember that," Paul said softly.

"All right, we have to set them up. He's screwing us around, Paul. But now that I finally know who he is I can –"

"Jon."

"I'm not going to kill him. Probably."

Paul hung his head a moment, rubbing his eyes. The long day had crept up on him. "How about we figure it out tomorrow?" he suggested.

Jon sighed. "I've been watching her, you know."

"Laura?"

"I took work off the other day and followed her."

Paul waited.

"She just shopped. That's all."

"Have you said anything?"

Jon flung his hands up. "What would I say? She's not going to admit it. God I hate this – I nearly punched a guy at work."

Paul shook his head. "Maybe you should talk to her then."

"Maybe." Jon glanced at his watch. "Why don't you stay here tonight? We'll figure out what we're going to do in the morning."

"Nah, I'm okay."

"It's fine, the guest room's made up. Go have a shower," Jon said as he stood, overriding Paul's objections and marching out of the room. He returned with a clean towel, which he threw at Paul with a grin. "I'll go tell Laura you're staying over."

Chapter 13

"Jon's been called in to the hospital. His mum's sick again but he said he'd give you a ring later." Laura handed him a cup of coffee. She wore a nightie that displayed much more skin than appropriate for a woman playing host to her husband's friend, but he said nothing. An image of her clinging to Grady came unbidden.

"Is she all right?"

Laura shrugged. "She's fine. I think she likes the attention, actually."

The kitchen was large; it had a modern look and benefited from a dozen little touches of colour, from utensils to small framed pictures and heat mats. From the other side of the room, she tied up her blonde curls then worked on her cup. He'd tried to leave early, but she was insistent. Laura would have felt she'd failed as a host if she didn't at least make him morning coffee, so he'd given up, taking a seat.

He sipped at his drink until she sat across from him with her own cup. "So, Paul, have you heard from Rachel?"

"No, not really."

"Hmmm. I haven't either. She usually jumps on the phone to text, usually once a day."

"How long has it been?"

She shrugged, and gave a titter, cheeks flushing. As if she were personally responsible for keeping tabs on Rachel – typical Laura, mothering everyone. "Weeks, I think. I, I've tried once or twice, and left a message but she hasn't got back to me and I've been so like a headless chook lately." She took another gulp of coffee and Paul noticed the nails on her hand had been chewed. "I still believe there's hope for you two. You're right for each other, you're quiet and she's cheerful, you know? Opposites and all that."

"I hope it's true. But I haven't heard from her in months, Laura."

"Oh." She paused. "Actually Paul, I've been meaning to ask you about Jon."

"Yeah?" He took an extra long sip.

Her sweet face frowned. "Does he seem...different to you?"

Like he knows you're cheating? "Not really, how do you mean?"

"More tense than usual. He won't talk much…about our… plans. For the future. I don't understand it. He forgot our ten year anniversary, I know he's a scatterbrain," she made a small gesture that seemed to both excuse and condemn her husband, "but he's never this bad."

"It's probably just work. You know how hard he works. He wouldn't have meant it," Paul said, knowing the words were empty, stupid even, but saying them anyway.

Laura nodded, voice flat. "I suppose so."

He took one more sip before standing. "I'm sorry to run.

The coffee was great, but I've got to get home and check on some things."

"You'll tell me if Jon says anything to you, won't you, Paul?"

"I will," he lied, moving for the front door as fast as he could while still acting within the scriptures of polite conduct.

At home he checked his messages, wandering the garden while he listened, giving cursory glances to the flower beds. More than a few plants needed attention, the hydrangeas seemed especially sad. He had a message from Mrs Greenhorne, who'd seen the police at his house yesterday, she wondered if everything was all right? "I don't know, but I doubt it," he told the answering machine. The police couldn't know what he'd done in Tobulla. It wasn't possible. Maybe they'd learnt something about Alessandra? But then, they wouldn't bother to tell him and it was more likely about something else he'd done – there was getting to be quite a list.

Leaning on the birdbath, he called Rachel again. Still no answer. What was going on? He went back inside and checked on his eBay store. There had been bids on a three-hundred dollar second edition of *The Hobbit* that he'd stumbled across at a garage sale, but it wasn't much of a thrill. He had to figure out what the hell to do. Jon would call when he was able, and the police were no doubt going to visit again. He moved to the piano and sat on the stool, opening the lid. Pressing a heavy key, he was surprised that the upright didn't sound too bad to his untrained ear. He thought it was seriously out of tune, but then, his father had always kept it in good working order. Paul pressed a few more keys. "What do I do now, Dad?"

Time for some air.

Locking up, he jogged through the breeze, heading toward the train tracks and the bridge, his feet taking him where he needed to go without his mind having to figure it out. At the bridge he slowed. A spot of blue peeked from beneath the stonework, caught in some undergrowth, its edges curling in the wind. He slipped down the slope and found the edge of a blanket. Deeper beneath the bridge, half-concealed, was a den of sorts. A second blanket had been laid across stones and a melted candle sat beside a canteen of water. The homeless weren't exactly unheard of in Stony Bay, but he rarely saw such acute evidence of them. Could this be where Alessandra was sleeping? There was no way to tell. He put the blanket back, trying to make everything neat and placed a rock on top, before crossing the bridge.

Toshiro wasn't home; no-one was, so he kept on to his uncle's. It took quite a while and it was well after lunch when he finally sat down to a glass of cold water, surrounded by the warm wood-tones of Henry's dining room. Henry put his orange juice down, same drink he'd had every day since giving up alcohol, rubbing at his wrists. "Well. What are you going to do? Jon will need to be careful."

"Yeah. And I don't know how serious this is. I'd check her work but according to Sarah Jennings she's taking time off... are you all right?"

"Just getting older." Henry gave his wrist one final rub and waved it off. "You know what you should do – visit Rachel yourself. Speak to her face to face, get that Grady out of the house. He works, doesn't he? Some sort of big shot in the city?"

"Yeah, he's a suit. Shares apparently."

"There you go. He's bound to leave the house in business hours."

"Yeah."

"So just go in there, see if Rachel is all right."

Paul got up and refilled his glass, unable to hold back a laugh, staring into the back yard as he did so. The curtains on Henry's window were wide open. Leaves swirled across a neat lawn. "I'm on thin ice with the police as it is. Breaking and entering won't look good in light of my other achievements."

"True, but you won't know if you don't try. How concerned are you?"

"Concerned."

"Then do it. Take Jon and make him stand watch."

He took out his phone. "Maybe."

"You know what I think." Henry stood, collecting wallet and keys from the bench. "I've got a dentist appointment to get to, so I'll let you lock up, all right? Let me know what you find. I wouldn't trust that Grady."

"You think he's done something to her?"

"I don't know, Paul. But I knew the Mayor when he was a boy, and he wasn't right. Bit of a cruel kid, mean to animals and the like." Paul opened his mouth, but Henry cut him off. "He could have grown up; some kids get over that sort of stuff. And some fathers don't pass on their bad traits to their children. So don't read too much into it, lad. I shouldn't have said anything, I suppose. I just think you're right to check on her."

"All right." Paul saw his uncle to the door, and dialled Jon's number.

Whether Grady was bad news or not, being unable to

contact Rachel was a little more than troubling. She was probably okay, she was flighty after all. It could have been a ploy, something she was telling Grady to do, act as a kind of screen for her. But then, why had she visited? It was beyond odd. After months of choosing not to, after finally making a step toward moving on by putting her from his mind and giving up any attempt to contact her, and after meeting Kelly too, one of the only bright spots in his life, Paul had been thrust back in time. All it took was a single visit, then her silence, and he was chasing her again.

Though her recent visit was a little different from the last one.

Jon answered, the hum of a car in the background. "Paul, I'm nearly at your place."

"Come to Henry's instead, Jon, I'm not home."

"Okay."

"We're going back to Rachel's place."

"I had the same idea."

*

Pink streaked the sky, blushing a bank of clouds where the sun struggled to keep its head above water. The ocean flew by, bright flashes between the trees. Jon didn't seem to be paying much attention to the speed limit.

"It's not a race."

"Yeah?"

"There's a bit of daylight left and he'll probably be home late," Paul said.

"I know. But I've had nearly all day to think about it. I don't want to run into him. I'll kill him." His friend's face was set. No trace of a smile, no hint of a joke. No blustering either. Jon was cold; his eyes never left the road and his hands were tight on the wheel.

"Jon..."

"I know it wouldn't help. But I'll tear that dog apart, Paul, if we see him."

"Then let's be quick."

"Yeah."

Impressions from last night were accurate, Paul saw, as they roared up the driveway toward their target. Grady's place was large – long-lying buildings with typically soulless modern architecture spread across manicured grounds, shielded from its neighbours by screens of trees and even a tall stone wall. It made the residence seem more of a compound, reinforcing the impression that they were breaking in.

"No cars," Jon noted as they pulled up in the gravel, circular driveway. "Does Rachel still own that little Toyota?"

"I think so. I can't see it, but."

Jon opened the car door. "Let's get this over with."

"What are you going to do? About Laura?" He followed Jon to the door, who pounded on the wood and waited.

"I don't know. I can't talk to her. I just keep picturing them together, or at least, her and...whatever...I don't really know what he looks like." He knocked again. "Fuck this, you wanna try another door?"

"Yeah." Paul led him around the side of the house, looking through the windows into a richly furnished place, with dull art on the walls and very sleek electronics; televisions, stereos and the like.

"What about that side door?"

Locked. Paul trampled flowers as he cut through the

garden and moved to the back door, which was also locked. "It's all locked," he called to Jon, who was jiggling a window.

"Find a bedroom."

Paul moved to a window and peered inside, but it was too dark. Jon waved him over to the next window and called through the glass, "Rachel? Are you in there?"

Paul added his voice. "Rachel, it's Paul and Jon. We're worried about you."

Nothing.

"She could be anywhere," he said. "This is a waste of time."

Jon grunted. "Give her another call; I'll see if I can get into the garage."

Paul dialled and once again, straight to voicemail. He left a second message and moved to the next window, pressing his face to the glass. The curtains, as with most of the windows, were drawn.

"Any luck?" he shouted to Jon.

His friend appeared at the side of the house, expression dark. "Paul."

"What?"

Jon led him to the double garage. The roller door had been pulled up and inside, surrounded by littered workbenches and racks of wine draped with spotty drop cloths, was a large shape covered by a green tarp. One corner had been pried loose, which Jon took and raised.

"It's Rachel's car."

"Take it off." Paul rushed forward to help Jon draw the tarp back, breathing hard. The car was empty. No convenient clues sat on any of the seats, nothing. He tried a handle but it was locked.

"Check the boot."

He gave Jon a look. "She wouldn't be in there."

"Let's be sure." He squeezed around behind the car before shaking his head. "Can't open it."

"Jon, don't be dramatic. He's not a murderer."

"Just let me check and we can move on."

Best to humour him. Even if there was no chance Rachel was... He rubbed his neck. "All right. Maybe the spare key's still here." Paul crouched beside the wheel and felt around until he found the magnetic key. His hand trembled as he fitted it to the lock. Jon was getting to him. She wasn't inside. She was fine. He turned the key and lifted the boot, jaw clenched.

A spare tyre.

"Empty," Jon breathed.

Paul shuddered as a chill ran across his skin, taking slow steps as he returned the key to its hideaway. "Why would he hide her car? And why put it in a garage and cover it with a tarp, when it's already out of sight?"

Jon grunted. "This guy's scum. He's cheating on your ex-wife with my wife, and maybe worse for all we know – the car proves everything."

"Everything?"

Jon strode forward, pointing at the house, and Paul realised that his friend was wearing gloves. When did he put them on? "We're going in there right now. Rachel might need us – you want to know what's going on, don't you?"

Paul nodded, following. Something wasn't right, that much was obvious. And yet... "The car could be broken down, you know. And I haven't called her father yet, she might be with him. At least, he might know something."

"Didn't you say he was overseas?"

"That's true." Paul kicked a shrub. "Damn it, Jon – where is she?"

Jon took off his jacket and wrapped it around his arm and fist. "Let's find out."

"Wait!" Paul reached out as Jon punched the window, the blow breaking but not shattering glass.

"Here." He took another pair of gloves from his jacket, handed them over and began pulling bits of the glass plane free. "Wear them."

"You knew you were going to break in?"

He gave a tight smile. "I thought we might have to. We might find something and if Rachel's locked up in there…"

"I don't think she's locked up, Jon."

"You said you thought Grady was lying and I agree. She could be in there because –"

"If she's sick she could be in hospital," he interrupted.

Jon shook his head. "That's what I'm trying to say. She's not in the hospital. I called."

"When?" Paul frowned. Why the hell hadn't he thought of that before?

"Earlier, from work. And now we know Grady is lying."

"Maybe she's just not home," he said, trailing off. Rachel wasn't in the hospital but that didn't mean she wasn't sick. Or that she was even inside.

"You don't believe that."

Paul rubbed at his eyes. The wren told him Rachel was in trouble, speaking through Brian the bird man. That alone was unbelievable enough – but there was the car too. And the phone calls. And her latest visit. She'd tried to tell him something. Why couldn't he trust all the signs? "I don't know anymore. None of this makes sense."

"Come on, Paul."

Paul crammed his hands into the gloves then paused. "What if he's got cameras?"

"Then the gloves won't make a difference. But I don't see any, do you?"

He pointed. "I meant in there."

"Come on." Unlatching the window, Jon slid it open. An alarm shrieked at his first step. He flinched. "Hurry."

Paul rushed after him, clomping into what looked like a guest bedroom. It was unused, a folded blanket on a chest at the foot of the bed the only hint of colour in the room.

"This is crazy," he shouted over the noise. "If we get caught, I'm screwed, you know that?"

"Just look around. We might find something then we can get out of here."

Paul dashed into a nearby room, Jon charging down the other end of a corridor. Storage. The kitchen was empty too – last night's dishes, enough for one, drying on a rack. He found a similar scene in the lounge, a leather armchair had a *Financial Review* on its seat and remotes were stacked on a coffee table. Empty.

He found Jon in the master bedroom, looking over the bed with a frown.

"Come on. This was a mistake." He took Jon's shoulder. "She would have heard the alarm."

Jon ignored him, crouching by the king-sized bed and overturning it with a shout. The mattress and frame crashed into the wall, toppling a bedside table and lamp as it fell back. The window didn't break, though it shook.

"Let's go." Paul led Jon back to the broken window, snatching at his friend as the man took off toward the garage. "What are you doing?"

"Help me." Inside, Jon grabbed a rag and wiped the car over while Paul worked on the tarp, affixing it as best he could. "That's it," he said, and ran to Jon's car, heart thumping as he pulled the seat belt on. "Go."

*

It wasn't until they'd nearly made it back to Mayfield Drive that Paul's ears stopped ringing. In the driveway, he massaged his temples until Jon killed the engine. "That was stupid, Jon."

"I dunno."

"It was."

"At least we know she's not there. I'd say she hasn't been there for a while. None of her clothes on top of the washing basket."

"You a detective now?"

"I just looked around. But I'm right, aren't I?"

"Maybe." Paul took out his mobile phone but stopped. "I'll try her again tomorrow – are you going to speak to Laura?"

"No idea. I think I wanna find Grady." Jon made a fist, examining his knuckles.

"Maybe wait a while? We just got away with something, let's not push it."

"Yeah."

Paul hauled himself out of the car and waved his friend off before trudging inside and collapsing into bed, kicking his shoes off with some difficulty. He knew pamphlets that came with new shoes warned against it, but who cared?

It didn't take long to fall asleep.

*

A knocking woke him. The house was dark and he made his way to the front door slowly, only switching on a light in the entryway. "Coming," he called, muttering unpleasant things as he stumbled. He rubbed his eyes and tried to straighten his rumpled clothing.

"Mr Fischer?" The man's face was Bogart-like, but he was blond and a little younger. An open jacket showed the tip of a pad sticking out of a shirt pocket, which he took out and opened. "Good evening, I'm Detective Clarke."

Paul's pulse marched double time. The break in, they knew. Somehow they knew. He rubbed his eyes to cover his pause. "Evening. Is there anything wrong?"

"No, sir. May I come in?"

Paul stepped aside, following the man to the kitchen. "Is this about Alessandra?"

"Pardon?"

"I mentioned her to Constable Stevens. She's a runaway."

"I see. Do you have something to share?"

"No. I haven't seen her for a while; she could be sleeping under the old bridge though. Maybe it's worth checking out." He gestured to the fridge. "Can I get you a drink?"

"I'll make a note of that sir, and water is fine, thank you."

Paul took a couple of glasses and filled them, handing one over. "So how can I help you, Detective?" He took a long drink, trying to quell the thumping of his heart, only it wasn't like hiccups and his pulse was still rally-car driving through his arteries when he placed the glass down.

"It's about a vehicle that was found at the bottom of Quartz Point."

Not the break in. "All right."

"A witness recalls seeing a man matching your description there on the day of the accident, about the time this luxury car was found."

Paul nodded. Everything had been worked out. "And you'd like to know if I saw anything?"

"I'd like to know why you were concealing your car there actually."

Who in God's name had seen him? "I was cycling. I used the Point as a halfway marker and I just wanted to find some shade for the car."

Detective Clarke made a sound, writing in his pad. "I'd consider placing branches over the bonnet and roof 'concealing', wouldn't you Mr Fischer?"

"I don't have air-conditioning. And anyone could have stolen my car if I left it in plain sight."

"Very well." He didn't sound convinced. "Did you see anything unusual there, either during your ride or when you returned to collect your car from its place in the shade?" The officer placed subtle emphasis on the word 'shade.'

"No." He took another drink.

"I see. Well, in light of your activities at Quartz Point and in addition your recent difficulties with Mr Maddocks, the intervention order in place at the request of your wife and the financial troubles you're facing with the closure of your store – and on top of which, your friendship with the owner of the very red Mustang that was destroyed, one Jon Levitan, I felt you should be given a chance to discuss the possibility that you stole then wrote the car off in order to help your friend scam his insurance company in exchange for a cut of the payout."

Paul offered no response. The man had obviously done his homework.

"Mr Fischer, would you like to accompany me to the station now?"

At least it wasn't the break in. "Let me get a jacket."

Chapter 14

Paul shivered, rubbing his hands together. The cell was exceptionally cold, as if ice blocks were hidden beneath the stone walls. Or maybe the evenly spaced bars were actually liquid nitrogen. Beyond the immediate confines of his accommodation in the Stony Bay Police Station, grunts and muttering came from the dim reaches of the opposite cell, and somewhere the officer on duty argued with the television.

He'd already left a message with Lloyd; there was nothing left to do but wait. He leant against the bricks and put his hands on his knees. The scent of old cigarette smoke lingered in his cell. Grand. Detective Clarke had been agitated when Paul refused to answer questions about the car or Jon. Instead, he limited himself to honest accounts of the more distant past – his separation and the intervention order, the assault and the collapse of his store. The 'lawyering-up' as it was described on cop-shows, didn't impress Clarke, but the man should have expected it. It was as good as an admission of guilt. Had Paul been a policeman he'd have thought so. But the candour he expressed in regard to his other transgressions seemed to confuse the detective a little. Whether that helped Paul or not, he'd no doubt find out later.

Waiting was about all Paul was good for now, that and breathing. He managed it quite well, dragging in as much air as his lungs could manage, holding it and releasing, not exactly meditation, but something of an attempt. He wrinkled his nose at the ever-present reminder of nicotine, but kept on until Lloyd's voice interrupted.

"If I knew you were good for it, Paul, I would say you were making me rich with all these indiscretions." He stood against the bars, his lined face tired. A lemon-yellow tie was undone at the neck. "But you are most convincingly broke."

Paul stood. "I'm out on bail?"

"Yes, as is your accomplice Jon. And I have another court date for you."

"Three to four weeks from now?"

"You are certainly getting to know the system well, Paul." Lloyd motioned to the duty officer, who was already fitting the key to the cell door. "May we go now?"

"Yeah, you're free," the man said.

Late afternoon sun turned Lloyd's old Kingswood orange. Paul hopped in, sliding on the bench-seat. The car had no CD player, not even a tape deck, but it had a radio which Lloyd had tuned to a country and western station. Johnny Cash was halfway through *Big River* when they pulled up to Paul's place.

"Thanks again, Lloyd. I really will pay you properly one day."

"I expect so. I am keeping a ledger, you know."

"Is Jon all right?"

"Perhaps, but he failed to say."

"Mmmm."

"He seemed well enough, though he looked tired. As I imagine we both do. Sleep is where we recharge, you know. Did I tell you I once slept for twenty-four hours straight after swimming the English Channel in 1973?"

"Ah, no, you didn't."

"Well I did. You should be impressed, by the way. Now, we should talk about our next step tomorrow. You will have an arraignment for something or other coming up soon, and then I suppose you will have to tell me all about your latest foolishness."

"I will. Thanks, Lloyd."

"Get some sleep, do you hear?" He held Paul's gaze a moment before turning back to the road.

An envelope waited on his doorstep, tucked beneath the welcome mat. Inside, he opened it on the way to the shower; first port of call as his skin was caked in nicotine, or it seemed. Kelly had called on him and had left something that, on any other night, would have perked him up. It was a photocopy, crooked but legible, of an e-mail from Martin Roberts to Maddocks, assuring him of Stony Bay Real Estate's cooperation in regards to 'moving certain unwanted business holders along' and expressing gratitude for a few perks at a toffee-mouthed Country Club.

"I expected no less from you, Roberts," he muttered, thanking Kelly as an afterthought as he placed it on the table. He read it again and slapped the wood. "Ha!" Roberts even suggested being more than willing to 'assist' in the rushing an unspecified 'rise' through on 'several Shell Street properties.'

Dialling his uncle's number, he left a message, explaining how little he'd achieved at Grady's. Next was Kelly, where he left another message. At the piano he ran his fingers across the black keys, pressing them at regular intervals but without rhythm or direction. Tomorrow was going to be a big day.

*

Once again, Rachel's phone went directly to voicemail and he left yet another message – it seemed to be all he was doing of late – and paced the backyard, broom in hand. Next he called Jon, who was in a meeting. "Not my day," Paul said, then took a moment to brush at cobwebs on the tool shed with his broom, not doing much of a job before dialling a third time – this time getting Kelly.

"Kelly, hi. I'm sorry I've been so hard to find." He leaned against the fairy wren's gum.

"It's fine, are you okay?"

"I've been in jail for a while."

"Jail? Oh God, what happened?"

"Nothing too serious. Can I tell you about it later, when we meet? I wanted to thank you for your package."

"All right, well I'm glad you got it at least. This morning I realised I probably shouldn't have left it there. Pretty stupid of me, anyone could have taken it."

"It all worked out. I gotta say, I'm impressed. How did you get it?"

"Easy. Roberts always asks me to check his computer when he thinks he's got a virus or something else he can't figure out."

"Wow. You did that for me?"

"Well, for everyone on Shell Street I guess, but for you, yeah."

He smiled. "Kelly, thank you. I don't know if it'll help me, it doesn't spell out exactly that Martin and Maddocks have something going on – but it definitely implies it. You're amazing."

"I know."

He laughed, but trailed off. "Wait. Are you risking your job? He'd know it was you."

"Maybe. You could always say you hacked in." She paused. "Paul, everything's not okay, is it?"

Paul looked up into the branches. "Can we talk tonight?"

"If you want."

"That'd be good," he said, her concern evident through the thin sound emitting from his mobile phone. "I've screwed up again, but I'll figure it out."

"All right, just...be home at seven, okay?"

"I will." He said goodbye and put his phone away. "What now?" he asked the garden. He had a chance at something good with Kelly, so long as he didn't blow it. If only the world wasn't about to spin off its axis.

Chirping drifted from a tree next door and he hurried over, but it wasn't the wren. "No offense little guy, but you're not who I wanted to see," he told the robin. What had happened to the fairy wren? He hadn't seen it since the day it somehow used Brian to speak. Was it hiding, resting? What had it taken to speak to him? Was there a chance it was with Rachel?

And what was the bird? A ghost? None of it made sense; he wasn't entirely convinced he hadn't been victim of some strange hallucination. Maybe he was insane, his mind reduced to a flickering set of splice-cut birds of brilliant blue, Italian runaways and large men in bird costumes. He paced the yard. And yet, it had happened. The bird was more than a bird. A guardian angel? He didn't buy that either; despite the comfort it might have offered.

Grady was lying, that much was clear. He didn't need an empty house for proof. Rachel needed help. She wasn't sick, it had to be more than that. And while not exactly his business anymore – and by law he wasn't allowed near her – he couldn't just leave it. Maybe she needed to know about Grady's betrayal? No. Paul tossed the broom aside. It was more than that, he wanted to find her. And it wasn't just obligation; maybe something of their love was left over from the shambles the marriage became. Maybe not much, but something. She needed help, and with her mother passed on and Alan overseas, there was no-one else. It was up to Paul. All of her friends had failed to return his messages. One slammed a door in his face and threatened to call the police. No way to know what they actually knew.

The fairy wren was trying to tell *him* she was in trouble.

But what exactly had the bird been doing in his tree?

Between the gum's branches lay a rough spot, largely indistinguishable from the ground. Glancing around for any curious neighbours, he leapt, caught a branch and scrambled up.

He froze when he reached the mark. An image of Rachel's face had been pecked into the tree. Deep jabs from the wren's beak formed the outline and detail of her face.

She wore an expression of terror.

*

Paul barged into Dr Alan Anderson's consultancy, the thick carpet almost slowing him. "Excuse me." He strode to the receptionist's officious desk. Working on her lipstick, a 'desperate-housewife' type glanced over her trendy glasses at him. More than a few patients waited in the office, their muffled coughs dominating the easy listening overhead. "Yes?"

"I need to contact Dr Alan Anderson, it's quite urgent. It's about his daughter Rachel."

"Oh. He's currently overseas, but he's due back to visit before the end of the year," she said, fumbling with some papers. "Who are you?"

"I'm her ex-husband," he said. "Paul Fischer."

"Oh, of course, I remember your name." She flashed a bright smile. "You won't believe this, Mr Fischer, but she's actually dating my brother Grady now. I introduced them, isn't that odd? Anyway, let me find those details for you." She disappeared to a back office, murmuring to herself about the contact details. "Here you go, Mr Fischer, that's his overseas number." She handed over a folded piece of paper. "I hope everything's okay. I know Rachel's been having a tough pregnancy and Grady's being so brave, but I know he's worried she'll lose the baby."

His stomach dived, Captain Nemo-like. When it hit the bottom he shot back up and surfaced with a single word. "What?"

"Oh, it's actually a little serious, I believe."

"A baby?"

"Yes. He's so happy, too."

"Where is she?" he managed.

"Home I imagine, but she's got to be close to giving birth, less than a week I'd say."

He tore his phone free and dialled as he ran from the building. Pregnant. After what she said...pregnant. Whose was it? Had she been seeing Grady back then? Or was that midnight visit something else?

It was his. It had to be. He'd never completed a mathematical estimate faster. The end of March – the end of November. It fit. The baby was his. That's what she'd been trying to say. He hadn't noticed because of the heavy coat. The baby was his. The coat threw him. It was his.

But if it was Grady's...

"Rachel, it's me, we have to talk, ring me back for Christ's sake," he demanded, slamming his car door and tossing the phone onto the passenger seat. Jamming the key into the ignition he slammed a fist into the wheel. "What the fuck is happening?" Not expecting an answer, he wrenched the shift into reverse and stomped on the pedal, ploughing into a red Lancer. "By God, fucking hell." The driver would have insurance; he didn't have time to leave a note. As he screeched from the car park, something trailed along the road. His rear bumper? It made a racket but he drove on, heading for Grady's house.

He would find her, find out what was happening. He would find her or tear the place apart, Grady included.

Chapter 15

The fairy wren stood in the middle of Grady's driveway, right where the gravel met the tarmac, preventing him from entering the property. Rain fell hard enough to keep his wipers busy. He inched forward and the wren hopped across, lining itself up with his wheel. He braked. "No. I know what you want now," he said, grabbing his phone and dialling Rachel's number. "Let me find her."

His wheels crept closer. Would the bird move? He lost it beneath the bonnet. "Come on." He hung up, tossed his phone aside and got out to crouch in the rain. The bird stood before his wheel. It looked up at him, dark eyes unblinking. He couldn't go any further. The wren wasn't going to shift; there was no hint of fear in its bearing. The head twitched, but it didn't move, waiting just centimetres from the front wheel.

"What is it?" The bird was hardly vibrant today, but it went further than poor light. The blue had faded, even the black feathers were duller. It was as if the wren had aged, or was being drained of colour. "Come on." He reached out a hand and the bird gave a shiver but didn't flinch, allowing him to cup it gently, wet feathers chill in his palm, it's little clawed feet hard. "You're too light, little guy."

It gave a thin chirp.

Paul started back to the car and the wren hopped and fluttered its wings inside his palm. He gave a cry when it pecked him, not too hard, but enough to escape. He leapt after it, but the bird was already flapping hard in the rain, settling on a security camera set on one of the flanking columns. Newly installed, it was probably not the only one; he wondered if it was even on?

Paul glanced up at the house. Would Grady even be home? The wren jumped into the lower branches of a tree, where it began to peck and hop. It flew to another tree, heading away from the property.

Rachel wasn't in the house; he already suspected that. "God damn it."

He'd trusted the wren before. He'd follow it now.

Paul backed out and tracked the wren from tree to tree, not driving too fast and not bothering to check on the bumper when it clattered to the road. He kept on toward town, ignoring the cars that passed, some with horns screeching. The fairy wren flew until trees gave way to the fields and houses, and finally shops. It flitted from eave to eave or sign to sign, skimming Subway and KFC, Office National and then the Stony Pub with its lattice veranda, where he'd once snuck a bottle from the bar. He headed out of town again, now toward the beach and eventually into a parking bay, where he startled a lone seagull perched on a rounded post. Wind pulled the door from his hand as he jumped out to chase the bird down a sandy trail lined with tea-tree. The roof of a small lifesaver's watch tower peeked over one of the dunes, but no-one surfed today.

Fireman's Beach was deserted. The trail ended in damp sand unblemished by footprints or driftwood, at least until he slogged through it to stop at the water's edge. The wren kept going, flying into an approaching storm. Below, the water chopped and crashed, whitecaps of displeasure topping every grey wave.

"Where are you going?"

The wren made little progress, fighting the wind, getting tossed around. Despite its struggle, it grew smaller beneath the black clouds. No normal wren could have managed the continuous flight it had taken just to reach the beach, but even the fairy wren looked to be in trouble. Lightning flashed out to sea, the rumble of thunder dull beneath the wind. The bird faltered. He took several steps into the chilly water, trying to keep it in sight, soaking his shoes. It didn't matter, the rain, heavier here, had already done a similar job on the rest of his clothes. It was madness, the wren was no match for the violence in the air, despite the pumping of its small wings it was being driven down. "Stop," he cried.

It disappeared beneath the waves.

Paul charged forward. He fought the tide until it reached his knees, where he dove into the darkness, slashing at the surface with his arms and kicking through water made thicker by his clothes. Heavy arms soon tired. He'd barely hauled himself to the bar when the swell tossed him off course. Changing direction was like moving the earth itself; the wind whipped rain into his face and he was no longer sure where the wren had dropped.

"No." The wren couldn't die; it was trying to tell him

something, to show him something about Rachel. Another wave crashed over Paul and he sucked in a breath when he surfaced. If only he'd climbed the tree sooner, he'd have seen the picture and visited Rachel before things got out of hand. Maybe if he'd tried harder to talk to her when she'd appeared that night. Then the bird wouldn't have had to lead him to Brian to get his attention, he wouldn't have wasted all that time. And now Grady had moved her and Paul was treading water, spitting salt and running out of strength.

Numb extremities struggled with clothes that had undergone an awful metamorphosis, turning from cloth to lead. He slipped under as another wave pummelled him. He had to turn back, he'd failed. His muscles burned as he swam for the shore, which was more distant than he remembered. Dragging strength from somewhere, Paul kept on, gradually becoming aware of a rushing sound – the sea was sucking him back, thunder raging. Over his shoulder the crest of a massive wave roared white and black. Paul had just a second for a chill, which had nothing to do with the cold, to ripple through his body, and then the monster was upon him.

*

Something stung his face. Paul opened his eyes to brightness and colour, blue and white resolving into the fragments of clouds, limping across a warm afternoon sun. Shivering, he leant over, coughing up sea water and sand, the grittiness of it covering his skin. The wind had done something to dry out his clothes, but they were still wet, just no longer water-logged.

"Oh, God." He'd survived worse than a brush with death. More of a long embrace. His chest was tender, as if the reaper's bones had dug into him.

Smooth sand stretched away to either side. He'd been washed ashore some distance from the path to the parking bay. Heaving his torso upright, Paul groaned at the pain. The water had been smoothed out by the warm hand of the sun, seaweed and new shells on the shoreline telling but little of the past fury. The wren was gone now. Its desperate flight cut short, his link to Rachel gone with it.

Paul slammed a fist into the sand, and kept doing it until he was breathless, wrenching himself up to a half sitting position. He was lost. Not just because of the wren. It was everything. He had one hell of a shovel. It seemed no hole was so big that he couldn't dig himself into it. His marriage, the store, Maddocks, everything. Every choice he made. Every step a wrong one, like an exquisitely poor move in a giant game of chess. Charging into the sea into the middle of a storm came to mind.

Every piece on the board hated him.

He had to try something else. Get control of his emotions. Maybe go to the police, confess everything and demand they help find Rachel – even if they proved him deluded, even if they proved that Rachel was fine? No. She wasn't fine and there no way they'd believe him anyway.

Paul wobbled to his feet and started back to the wagon, hand throbbing from his attack on the sand. Halfway there, a flash of metal stopped him. Washed up on the shore, caught in a tendril of seaweed was an odd shape. He stumbled over, shoes squelching. A trumpet lay in the sand. He looked to the ocean, then to the dunes, but saw no shipwrecked Titanic, no mournful busker, no dazed high school band, nothing that would explain the instrument's presence on

Fireman's Beach.

Its brass colouring was unblemished by rust and he blinked when he picked it up. A small, white shape lay curled inside the bell. It was almost translucent, like a jellyfish, but bones were visible, and what could have been a skull lay nestled over the chest. "A beak." Paul swallowed. The breeze teased a single puff-like feather from the bell, a trace of blue in its white.

Tipping the trumpet, he let the wren fall into his palm. It was not a skeleton, but the colour had been drained from its body. A milky white was still visible in some places, partially obscuring tiny internal organs, but no more blue and no more black.

The fairy wren.

The eyes were closed but the faintest pulse struggled against the skin. He had to get it somewhere warm. Taking a translucent bird to a vet, with a story about finding it in a trumpet that had washed up from the ocean, was not going to get him far, and who knew how much time the wren had left? Home. Placing it back into the bell, he jogged through the sand to his car and leant the trumpet against the wheel, keeping it upright while he searched for his keys. Nothing. His wallet was gone too, lost to the ocean.

"Damn it." Managing a lurching sprint back to the beach, he searched the sand but found nothing. It had been a long shot, and he had a spare key beneath the back wheel. As for his wallet, the cards could be replaced and whatever little cash had been inside wouldn't help him now.

Once he was on the road, the heater blasting and the wren in its brass cocoon on the passenger seat, where his mobile phone still rested, Paul released a long-held breath.

Adrenaline still surged through his veins, using them for a liquid Dakar. The wren could expire at any moment for all he knew. That it was alive now made no sense but it had a heartbeat. It had a beat – it had a chance.

Crossing town on streets that avoided traffic lights and stop signs, he was home in short order, charging across the driveway with trumpet in hand, coming to a halt at his front door. No keys. He ran to the back shed, emptied a soup tin of nails and grabbed his spare. Once inside, he kicked off his shoes and went to the laundry, grabbed a towel and placed the wren inside, dabbing at its feathers and resting the makeshift nest before one of his heaters.

"Come on, little wren." He dripped on the carpet. It didn't stir but when he rested a fingertip on its chest, the heart was quivering. Was it stronger? He waited. The beat didn't falter, but it didn't seem to be much stronger. Holding his own hands to the heat, he gave it a little longer before stripping down himself and showering, washing the sand from his hair and finally putting an end to his shivering. Steam and hot water eased the tension in his body and he leant against the tiles a moment. If the wren hadn't been so close to death, he would have stayed longer.

Wearing just his own towel, he returned to the wren. It hadn't regained any colour but still had a pulse. What else could he do? It wasn't moving; he couldn't try feeding it. The best he could manage was to try and keep it warm. When night fell nothing had changed and between one moment and the next, he fell asleep.

He woke with a dry mouth and a runny nose, slumped in an armchair he'd pulled over by the heater, after first lowering the settings. The wren was alive, or at least, it seemed to be. The heart, partially visible inside the towel, gave weak but consistent pumps. "Are you in a coma, little guy?" After most of a day and all night, its condition hadn't changed at all, except to become dry. Paul supposed it was safe enough to take his eyes off it for a time. He'd already showered and fallen asleep and nothing went wrong. The initial panic gone, more mundane things like food became important.

He sneezed as he prepared breakfast. How generous of the sea – a dip in the ocean and a cold to go with it. Paul found a tissue, then started with an overripe banana in yogurt, glancing at the wren as he worked on toast to follow up. Checking the store's site could wait, Jon probably couldn't. Who knew what he'd been up to? And finding Rachel, how would he do that? Now that the wren was comatose, going back to Grady's was an option. But checking other hospitals in the area might be better. The wren couldn't help him; he didn't know if he could even leave it, or what it would mean if the bird died. What did it know about Rachel? She was in trouble, everything pointed to that. If only you could talk, little wren.

A fragment of his dream struck him as he chewed, almost like a flashback. A wolf, fangs wet with blood, twirled with Rachel in a dance hall. Glen Miller conducted in the background, his glasses fractured. Her face glowed and she laughed her way through the steps, gripping shaggy paws. The wolf did nothing but stare over its shoulder at him, as if Paul were in the hall with them. One of its eyes was a camera, its lens making constant adjustments in focus. Beneath the music, he'd heard a thumping on a door, and someone called his name.

Paul shook his head and went through the routine of

dressing and preparing for the day, even taking an old licence from a drawer, just in case, though it was all hypothetical at this point. What was he going to do? Carry the bird in its trumpet to every hospital in the area? They'd think he'd escaped from the pysch-ward. But that was where she had to be, Paul could count. She'd be due soon, and if she was ill as well as heavily pregnant, she'd be in a hospital. Jon wouldn't have called maternity. She might even be in labour now.

And Grady the slime-bag – what was his game? If he wasn't the wolf from the dream, Paul was the fairy godmother from Cinderella. The puffed-up little prick was hiding her, but why? Did he know the baby might not be his? That all depended on when he and Rachel started dating. Alan would have to know where she was – he should have called the man earlier. Finding the number the receptionist gave him; he grabbed the house phone and dialled, glancing at the clock. Eight in the morning. Probably getting close to midnight in America. "Hope you're awake, Dr Anderson." He pressed the keypad.

The dial tone stretched on. The moment before he was sure it would stop, Alan answered, his tone curt. "Dr Anderson speaking."

"Alan, it's Paul, I need to know where Rachel is."

A slight delay followed his words, then Alan's blustering came through. "Paul, do you have any idea what time it is here? This is beyond ridiculous."

"Yes I do, but it's important. I need to speak to her, Alan – did you know she was pregnant before you left?"

"She told me, Paul. I've known for some time. Now, does this really concern you? I have an early morning. I simply don't have time for this."

"The baby's probably mine, Alan," he snapped.

A long silence followed. When he next spoke, Dr Anderson's voice was laced with ice. "Paul, I thought you'd grown up after the mature way you were handling the divorce. But this is a poor excuse for a trick. Rachel did not tell me you were the father. What she told me, was that she didn't want to see you. Why can't you accept that the relationship is over? Get on with your life, boy! And, Paul? Don't call this number again."

Dr Anderson hung up. Paul slammed the phone onto the bench top and dialled again. Engaged. Alan had pulled the phone from the wall, or left it off the hook. Paul paced. There had to be another way to find her. Something he'd overlooked. The GPS in her phone was useless, it'd been switched off for days. Her car at Grady's house told him nothing. Perhaps it was time to visit the man at work.

Someone rapped on the front door, a faint echo of his dream. "Mr Fischer, open up. This is the police."

"What now?" he hissed, before admitting Detective Clarke and Constable Stevens, taking them to the kitchen and offering them a seat and a drink. Both were refused. "Mr Fischer, when was the last time you saw Grady Dolan?"

"A few nights ago when I tried to visit Rachel."

"Your silver Mitsubishi Magna was seen at his estate yesterday."

"Yes, but I didn't go inside so I didn't see him. Why do you ask?"

"And what were you doing there, sir?" Stevens asked.

Here it comes. They're leading up to the break in. "I wanted to see Rachel; we have something to discuss."

"Which would violate your intervention order."

"Yes it would."

Stevens blinked and Detective Clarke took over. "And what of your ex-wife then, when was the last time you saw her? Why did you need to speak to her?"

"We have personal business to discuss, in regards to her pregnancy. I last saw her when she came to my house, about three weeks ago. She left before we could speak, as I had company."

Clarke raised an eyebrow. "And what time was this?"

"About tea time. Look Detective, why are you asking me all these questions?"

"That ought to be obvious, in light of your well-documented obsession with Rachel Anderson, who is known to be currently living with Grady Dolan."

"Well-documented?"

"You appear to have been calling her mobile multiple times a day for several days now, and there is the Order."

"I explained that. Her pregnancy does indeed concern me because I believe I'm the father. And I'm sorry but I can't help that. I'd actually appreciate any information about where Rachel is, if you come across something. I'm worried about her."

Detective Clarke paused, seeming to change what he'd been going to say. "We will certainly try, Mr Fischer."

"Thank you."

Clarke moved toward the door, trailed by his Constable, but paused with a hand on the knob. Paul tensed, here it was. The break in. "Actually, there is one more thing. Your friend Jon Levitan. I wonder if you've heard from him?"

"No. We haven't spoken for a couple of days. Why? Is he

missing too?"

"We're not sure, but if you have any information we expect to hear from you." He paused. "And Mr Fischer? Don't leave Stony Bay."

"I wasn't planning to."

"Good day, Mr Fischer," Clarke said. Paul exhaled as he watched them climb into a dark blue car and drive off. He understood now. Maybe Grady's cameras knew who'd broken in, but the man hadn't reported the break in. If he did, the snake would have had to face questions about Rachel.

Finally a piece of luck.

He checked on the wren. It hadn't changed, a faint pulse still blinked beneath its translucent skin. If it would just get better, he'd be able to find her. Paul moved it away from the heater and picked up the trumpet, pressing the keys in a random pattern and continuing to pace.

Chapter 16

When he finally went to check his phone in the magna, Paul found it overflowing with messages. Three were from Kelly, who'd been to visit him last night, as promised, and he'd slept through it. Nothing had roused him. She'd even pounded on the back door and his bedroom window. She was pissed off; he could hear it in her voice, despite the patience she was trying to show. He'd make it up to her somehow, but he couldn't just yet. In fact, the less he spoke to Kelly the better for her.

The messages from Jon gave him a chill that turned his bones brittle.

He pressed the keypad to replay the last message, to be sure he'd heard properly. "Paul, answer your fucking phone! I need help, I've done something stupid. It's Grady – I've killed him. Call me back for fuck's sake; I don't know what to do." It was one of the calmer messages, left just an hour ago. The others started late last night, and were frantic with cursing, shouting and garbled sentences.

Paul deleted them and collected the fairy wren, wrapped

in its towel-nest, and sprinted to the car. He scratched the door as he fumbled with the spare key and once inside, he laid the wren on the passenger seat and reversed out of the driveway, phone in hand.

Alessandra stood in the middle of the road. He stomped on the brake. She ran around to his window, shouting his name.

"What's wrong?"

She answered in Italian, pointing to the seat beside him then running round and opening the door, where she grabbed the towel before jumping in. "*Sbrigati*," she hissed, cradling the wren, "*sbrigati, sbrigati*." He lurched from the driveway, heading out of Mayfield Drive.

"What's wrong?" He drove with only half his attention on the road. Alessandra kept glancing over her shoulder with wide eyes, breathing hard, as if she'd been running. She hadn't noticed the see-through bird in her lap.

"*Uomo*," she said.

"A man? Chasing you?"

Again, her answer made no sense. Glancing in the rear view mirror, there was no evil-looking men in the street, nothing more than a couple of cars. He kept driving, pushing a little hard on the pedal, heading toward the caravan park Jon mentioned in one of his frantic messages. Alessandra was still talking, but all he could say in response was that she'd be all right. He had no idea if that was true – he was taking her to a situation that wasn't safe for him, let alone a runaway from Italy. But how could he just leave her there? She was upset, her face was tear-streaked and she was thinner than before. He had to do something.

As long as he kept driving, she seemed calm enough,

looking over her shoulder only rarely. He didn't call Jon, not knowing whether it'd spook her again. When he finally drove into Three Hills Caravan Park – crawling past the small office with its 'Back in Five Minutes' sign – his shirt clung to his back and the hair at his temples was damp with sweat. Murder. How in the hell had it come to murder?

The park was as spacious as it sounded, spread along the coast with sites for fixed and mobile vans, as well as cabins closer to the water. It was well-tended too. The right amount of green grass on the inch-tall grounds, paved walkways and decorative elms that spread shade for cautious outdoor-types. An officious sign gave the requested speed limit, five kilometres per hour, which he stuck to dutifully, not wanting to draw the attention of holiday makers in their shorts and thongs, their faces unbearably happy. Kids laughed and chased each other; older ones kicked the footy on the lawn or sat by the water, shoulders touching. He caught the scent of barbequed sausages and eggs as he drove deeper, heading for a distant cabin. Alessandra left off her questions, none of which he understood, at the scent of food. If the words 'aiding and abetting in the disposal of a body' weren't going round in his head, he supposed he would have asked one of the families for a bite for Alessandra.

Instead, he drove beyond the caravans and their awnings, pulling up before cabin ten, Jon's dark BMW out front. Set away from most of the others, the cabin was big, built of brown weatherboard with a porch and broad windows with drawn curtains. He had no idea how Jon had managed to get such a cabin this close to the holiday season. No, he did know. The man had probably bribed the owner or something, and a one-time happy family was now no doubt crammed into tighter accommodations. Beyond its small, fenced garden, screened by trees, was a second fence, this one serving as a partial barrier to the beach. Sand and water lay beyond, but there was no-one on the beach here, nor did anyone appear at the door when he pulled up.

"Alessandra, can you stay here?" He pointed to the car several times. "Stay here for a while."

She nodded, and didn't complain when he took the towel from her and placed it on the back seat. Knocking on the door to cabin ten, he called softly. "Jon, it's me." Footsteps crossed the room inside and the door opened a crack. Jon's unshaven face was revealed, and he flung the door wide. "God, Paul, thank god." The man's voice was strained, transformed into a kind of Miles-Davis rasp.

"What happened?" Paul hissed. Jon's eyes were red; his hair wild. Bloodstains marred his shirt and jeans. The interior of the cabin was little better, even if Jon looked to have made some effort to clean up; straightening a table and a chair, though one of the legs was splintered and something had been spilt on the carpet. A broken painting of a seascape was stacked against a corner but fragments of it remained stuck in the rug. Scuff marks covered the linoleum floor and shattered glass crackled under his feet.

"Jon, what happened here?"

He frowned over Paul's shoulder. "Who's the kid in your car?"

"The Italian runaway. I nearly ran her over on my way here."

"Will she keep quiet?"

"She doesn't speak English and she's staying in the car. Look, she's singing or something." Alessandra's voice reached him, sweet and low, the words indistinct.

"He's in the back." Jon took him to a thin-looking door leading to a bathroom, where a figure lay crumpled in the shower. A blanket covered his form, only the hint of a foot was visible beneath one edge. Paul's stomach flipped. A muteness seeped from the body, one that went beyond what he thought possible. The absence of life filled the room, pouring from the shape in waves. It wasn't like a person in a deep sleep, or even a coma, like his grandfather before he died. There was not even the suggestion of life. It could have been a pile of vegetables, boxes or toys beneath the blanket.

Instead the remains of Grady Dolan, Mayor's son, Businessman, Adulterer and whatever else he was, were crammed into a shower and taking their first cold steps toward decomposition.

"I stripped him and I was going to bury him, or maybe get him out to sea somehow, I dunno. Should have done it last night, but I wasn't thinking."

"Are you now?" Paul asked, without turning from the blanket.

"Fuck it, Paul."

"Yes you have, you've fucked it for both of us, haven't you?" Paul roared, shoving his friend into the wall. "What the hell are we going to do now? Everything else I thought I could deal with, but not this." He flung an arm at the corpse.

Jon's bewildered expression didn't help. Paul kicked a hole in the plaster and stormed to the kitchenette where he ran his head under the tap, still shivering. When he was done, he slammed a fist onto the sink, rattling dishes. He fought down vomit, somehow keeping it together enough to face Jon and ask another question. "How?"

The bigger man leant against the fridge and ran his hands over the front of his jeans. "I texted him, from Laura's phone. I took it yesterday, before she went to work. I told him we should meet somewhere new, suggested here. He fell for it. It was too easy; the filthy prick was keen for it."

"But you killed him."

He kept on. "When he got here and found me instead of Laura, he tried to run back to his car. Little fuck. I caught him before he had the door open and dragged him back inside, got to work." He rubbed his knuckles. "After a few minutes of it, he was in bad shape so I stopped. Tried to get some answers out of him, you know? About Laura and Rachel. I was just going to hold him here until I could call you and we could figure out what to do. But he was a smart-mouthed little prick. He told me about…the things he and Laura did. They'd been fucking around behind my back for nearly a year. She's getting ready to leave me, Paul." His tone of voice was disbelieving. It darkened. "So I finished it. I shut him up. I kicked his teeth in and stomped on his throat until his face went black." Jon gave a shudder and began to dry retch, staggering for the sink. Paul got him a glass of water, which Jon gulped down. "I, I had to cover his face; I couldn't look at him anymore. It took me an hour to undress him; I threw up a couple of times. God, oh god, I…" He fell silent a moment, putting the glass down. "His clothes are in a plastic bag somewhere. We'll have to get rid of them too."

Paul found the bag stuffed behind the toilet, and placed them beside the shower, trying not to look directly at the body. "We should wait until dark to move him," Paul said when he found Jon in the lounge room. A stupid thing to say, but he had to say something, had to make some sound.

The empty look in Jon's eyes was too much. This was Jon the joker, ever capable, always relaxed. Now he was like a corpse himself.

"Yeah."

"You have to clean up too – I'll bring you some clothes."

"Don't be long."

Paul returned to check on Alessandra, who was still singing to herself, a small smile on her face as she enjoyed the breeze. The girl was full of surprises, not too long ago she'd been frantic. "We have to come back." He pointed to the cabin. "Later, back here to this...*casa*," he said after a moment.

She nodded and made no objection as he crossed town and pulled up at his house again, rushing inside. Alessandra followed, going straight to the kitchen cupboard and rummaging around. Paul left her while he gathered a tarp, shovels and rope from his shed. At least his nose had cleared. He went into the bedroom and found a shirt that was a little too large for him, some of his loosest jeans and socks and a pair of Blundstone boots he used for gardening. Jon had screwed it all up. Finding Rachel was going to be impossible now. Still on his knees in the cupboard, he began to slam the Blundstones into the carpet, over and over until a voice stopped him.

"Paul?"

Alessandra stood behind him, holding the towel in her hands, mouth slightly open and eyes wide. He dropped the boots into the bag of clothes he'd found and joined her. Inside, the fairy wren was blushed with blue. Its heart beat stronger and the eyes were open, though it still didn't move.

They exchanged a look. "Amazing."

"*Incredibile.*"

"Come on, Alessandra." He gathered everything and loaded the car. Alessandra helped him, adding the trumpet to the pile. Why, he couldn't guess, just felt the need, but it didn't matter. It would probably give her something to do while she was waiting, as he didn't have time to drop her anywhere. He'd have to risk taking her along again. The wren too. It was too precious to leave alone.

On his second and final trip to the car, Alessandra and wren behind him, he was confronted by a glaring man dressed in slacks and a white business shirt. It matched his complexion, he was a pasty-looking guy with receding hair. Expecting another lawyer, Paul gaped when the suit pointed a finger at Alessandra and began shouting and spitting. 'There you are' was all the English he heard, the rest was in Italian, but more than a few swear words were in there.

And something odd...*ragazza demone*...Demon-girl?

What the hell was wrong with this guy?

Alessandra shrank back behind Paul, who blocked the man when he stepped after her. The fellow went bug-eyed. "Who the hell are you?"

"You first."

"I'm her father, that's who I am, you bloody paedophile. Now get out of my way, I'm taking the little freak home." He reached to drag Paul aside, but Paul broke his grip.

"Not like this you aren't."

"Out of my way."

"No."

The man turned his back, tugging at his hair, as if he couldn't believe someone was standing up to him. Then he swung, putting his shoulder into the blow. Paul was ready.

With one hand he pushed Alessandra back a step and with the other he deflected the man's swing.

He blustered, and Paul gave him a shove, more of a warning. "On your bike."

"Give her to me, she's my bloody daughter."

"I said 'no'."

He charged and Paul moved back, letting the man overextend himself, catching a wrist and sending the guy crashing to the concrete driveway. Winded, Alessandra's father struggled to rise, but Paul was on him before he could roll over, pressing a heel on the man's chest. "Leave now and I won't give you a thrashing."

"She's my –"

"Leave," he snapped, putting pressure on the man's sternum until he nodded. Paul hauled the scumbag to his feet and gave him another shove.

"I'll be back with the cops, you hear me?"

Paul took a single step. The man scrambled across the road and jumped into his car, pulling his mobile as he drove off. Alessandra clung to him, burying her face in his shirt and squeezing him with her free arm. He stroked her hair. "You're all right."

Mrs Greenhorne ran across the street, her face alight with a mix of concern and what Paul suspected was suppressed excitement. No doubt the news of what had happened would very soon be flying up and down the street on telephonic wings, if it wasn't already. But no-one else came out. She greeted Alessandra, who'd placed the wren in the car, before taking Paul's arm. "I just saw, oh my, Mr Fischer. That man, was he her father?"

"Yes."

"And what you did to him, it was most unexpected."

"He did attack me."

"Oh, I know, I know, he did at that. So it's probably true then. He is abusive to her."

"It seems so."

She wiped at her brow and pushed her dyed curls back into place. "Are you heading out? You see, I could look after Alessandra for you."

He considered it. Everything would be easier without Alessandra, but he didn't want to leave her behind. Or expose Mrs Greenhorne to any further trouble, either from the police or from Alessandra's father. "Thank you but I'll keep her with me until I can get in contact with the police. I don't want him to come back, he might give you trouble."

"Oh, well, yes that's true. Perhaps it is best." She paused, a frown creasing her forehead. "What shall I tell the police when they arrive?"

"That I'm taking Alessandra to a restaurant for a meal. *DiFranco's.*"

Back in the wagon, Alessandra hummed along to a song only she could hear, this one subdued. Her shoulders were slumped but Paul had to concentrate on his breathing before he could check on her, trying to work the adrenaline out of his system. Sending the police to a restaurant had to buy some time at least, make sure he wasn't followed. But surely he was in the clear? Even if the police left the moment they got a call from Alessandra's father, they would miss him take Lafayette Street and head toward Three Hills. But they'd be watching his house now all the same, with both Grady and Rachel missing, and now this. They'd have no choice.

"Alessandra," he started, speaking softly. "Do you still

have your book, *libro*? Calvino?"

"*Si.*" Still holding the wren, she reached into her bag and held up the book he'd seen when he cooked chicken for her.

"*Bene.*" It might give her something else to do while he and Jon worked; who knew how long it would take? And maybe he could get her some more food, she was probably starving. He'd only seen her munch on a few biscuits before she brought him the wren.

Pulling into Three Hills and rolling up to Cabin Ten, he asked Alessandra to stay in the car and read, doing his best to explain what he wanted. Rushing inside, he found Jon showered, pacing in a towel. He still looked lost, but accepted the clothes readily enough. The shirt looked a tight fit, but everything else was good enough. "What now?"

"Now we find Alessandra something to eat and wait for dark. Is there a TV in here?"

Jon pointed to the wall opposite the couch.

"Good. We'll put her in front of that. Can you manage to get us some food? I lost my wallet and I haven't had a chance to get new cards or anything."

"I can do that."

"Good. I'll make sure she doesn't go into the bathroom until it's cleaned up."

"Shouldn't we...roll him up first? Or dig the hole?"

"I brought a tarp. You don't want to put him in the ocean?"

Jon shook his head. "We'd have to find a boat."

"Good point. I brought shovels just in case."

He nodded, lumbering toward the door. "I'll get that food then, there's a little kiosk behind the office."

Paul made sure the door to the bathroom was closed, refusing to look inside, and brought Alessandra into the house. The shovels, rope and tarp could wait until dark. Seating her in a chair, he found some water and let her read, something she seemed happy enough to do until Jon returned, food in arms, something that helped with the introductions.

While Jon took Alessandra into the kitchenette to organise the food, Paul checked on the wren. Alessandra had placed the fabric nest on a small round table that stood by the television cabinet. Its chest rose and fell and while the bluish tinge hadn't faded away, it didn't appear any stronger. Its wings had more definition and the head was a little darker, but its eyes were closed now. He brushed a finger across its back. A shiver ran up his arm and hard on its heels came an image. It flickered like a hand-wound camera with several slides missing, black squares alternating with an image of Rachel lying on a bed. Light from a small window fell across her swollen stomach where it rested beneath a thin sheet. Sweat coated her face but she slept. A bottle of water sat on a nightstand but the rest of the room was reduced to vague shapes; he could just make out teddy bears on the wallpaper near the closed curtains.

He fell back when it ended, sitting until the dizziness passed.

Where was she? It didn't look like a hospital.

"What do we do now?" Jon asked, moving over to the door. Alessandra sat next to Paul and chomped on a salad roll. The vision faded, but he held on to it, filing it away for later. Murder. The word wasn't going anywhere. Grady crammed into a shower, covered up. How long before the body began to smell? Shame oozed from the walls, Cabin Ten had seen it. Could wooden panel walls flinch?

"Wait until dark to bring in the rope and tarp, wrap him up and get the hell out of here."

"Into the bush?"

"Yeah, somewhere secluded. We have to make sure no-one finds him. Ever."

"I know a place. We'll take my four wheel drive."

Paul tried not to think. "All right."

He switched the television on and did his best to watch a *Magnum PI* rerun, but he couldn't focus, couldn't smile, even when Higgins, true to form, lost it at Magnum over the Ferrari. He channel-surfed while Jon paced or ate potato chips, and even walked around the small yard when the idea of Grady Dolan's corpse in the next room became too much. He used the time to show Alessandra where the toilet blocks were, managing to get through the hours until darkness with only a supreme effort of will. Cancelling his credit cards wasn't much of a distraction and if he hadn't have been able to watch Alessandra attempt to teach Jon some Italian, it would have been a hell all the more painful for its mixture of boredom and terror. As it was, his head spun at every car engine, checking the windows often to see if the police had found them.

At times, he thought he caught a scent of the body. But he didn't open the door and when full dark came, he put Alessandra and the wren straight into his car, miming that she close her eyes. He had no idea how long she'd comply, but the girl agreed. Next he backed Jon's BMW as close as possible to the door and the two of them manhandled the corpse into the boot, first checking that none of the families were out and about. Jon closed the boot then caught Paul's shoulder. "I have to clean up."

"Shit."

"Take Alessandra somewhere and meet me at my place."

"You sure?"

"Yeah, this is my mess. Go on."

"Jon –"

"Don't waste time. We've got a long night ahead of us. This won't take me too long. I hope."

Paul jogged to his car and got in, resting his hands on the wheel a moment. He closed his eyes, not moving until Alessandra spoke. He turned the key.

Chapter 17

Paul gave Mayfield Drive a wide berth, certain Detective Clarke would be waiting in some sort of stake-out cliché. Instead, he dropped Alessandra off with Anton, arriving as the man was just sitting down to dinner. The short man shook her hand, exchanging a flow of words that put her at ease. He glanced at Paul, before taking her to the table, where she dug in, a big smile on her face. Anton's family spread around a large, overburdened table. Everything smelt wonderful, it was the only detail he registered, giving Anton's wife half a wave as the man pulled him into a dim lounge room. A Christmas sale blathered away on the television, its brightness utterly inappropriate for Paul's mood.

"Paul, what's going on?"

"I need you to explain something to Alessandra for me."

"Okay."

"Just let her know I'll be back, but that it'll take a few hours, and that her father doesn't know where she is. Can you do that?" He gripped the man's arm. "Anton?"

"Yes, yes, Paul don't worry about her, all right? She'll be

fine here." He frowned. "But Paul, she told me you and Jon are up to something."

He swallowed. "Yeah?"

"She doesn't know what, but she said it was something bad. Are you all right?"

He shook his head. "Smart girl."

"Paul."

"The less you know the better, Anton. But we're safe and so are you, her father doesn't know where she is. Just wait for me, all right?"

"All right." He gave Paul a look before seeing him out.

Paul had left the wren in the wagon and he checked on it before heading to Jon's, brushing a fingertip across its wing. Nothing happened. Relief, disappointment, he didn't know. At least it didn't look any worse. Paul fell into the uneven routine of switching his beams from high to low. The passenger seat felt empty without Alessandra there.

He laughed. How ridiculous it was, that every time he convinced himself things weren't getting worse, something proved him hideously wrong. Thanks, Jon, next time kill Maddocks. Make life easier for a change. Paul clenched his jaw. Grady probably could have told him where Rachel was. Now he had nothing. He was cursed – all his fuck-ups had just been topped but here he was like an obedient moron, helping dispose of a body. The police would catch them. Murder wasn't for beginners. They'd make a mistake somewhere. Paul sneered. That's all he'd been doing lately anyway.

Jon was already home when Paul pulled up in the dark. He left the wren on the passenger seat and hopped out. "You done?"

"I cleaned enough for now. I'll go back tomorrow and finish it; I paid for tomorrow night too, just to be sure."

Paul grunted. "What if someone goes in now?"

"I've put a 'do not disturb' thing on the door. That's all I could think of. We don't have enough time for anything else."

Paul looked to the house. "Where's Laura?"

"Don't know, but she's not home so let's be quick."

"Fine." He strode to the BMW's boot.

Jon caught his arm. "What's with you?"

"What do you think? You're going to get me thrown into jail, Jon – and how am I supposed to find Rachel now?"

Jon made no response, instead turning to his car and taking one end of the body. Fine, Jon. Let's not talk. Paul helped him transfer the corpse to the four wheeler, added the shovels and got in. He tried to wipe the feel of Grady's shoulders from his hands. The body weighed a tonne, without Jon it would have been hard to move. It was hard enough *with* Jon. His friend drove out of town, heading away from the coast. After about half an hour he turned off the highway into dense bush, eucalypt crowding other species that lined their way. Jackson's Road looked well-used, but leading from that, winding deeper into the bush, was a dirt trail obviously favoured by four-wheel drive joy-riders. In the powerful beams of Jon's Jeep the wooden sign read 'Longford Track'.

He could imagine himself denying knowledge of each one. Jackson's Road? No, haven't been there. Don't know where it is, same with Longford Track. Not much of an outdoors man actually, Officer.

"Jon."

"Huh?" Jon was chewing his lip, eyes shadowed in green light cast from the dashboard.

"This isn't right."

"I don't give a fuck. No way I'm going to jail for that prick."

"Shit, Jon. Look at what we're about to do."

He slammed on the brakes. Dust curled around the headlights. "So what's your big idea, Paul? How you gonna fix this? You can't, neither of us can."

"I know that," he snapped. "I just don't like it, do I?"

"So let's just get this done."

"I'm here, aren't I?"

"Then come on. I need your help, Paul."

Paul waved at the dark road before them. "Fine."

When Jon finally stopped, it was by a sluggish stream that was more a murmur than any particular colour. Tiny flashes caught on faint ripples and the trees loomed, bark going from black to pale grey when Jon pulled the vehicle into position so that the lights shone on a patch of ground before the water.

"This the place then?"

Jon nodded. "The ground should be softer here."

"What if we just throw him into the stream?"

"Too shallow."

"A ravine?"

"I know this place and we're here now, with a lot of work to do. Besides," Jon added, getting out and grabbing one of the shovels. "A hiker might see a body in a ravine."

"Right."

His footfalls hissed through the grass as he took his own shovel. A cloak-like silence pressed in around them, silence that wasn't truly silent but more an absence of sounds common to the towns and cities. No cars, no buses creaking, no slamming doors, rattling of fence pales, no bee-hive mush of conversation spiked by shouts or laughter, no music drifting from neighbours or shops, no chink of spoons on mugs. Just the accusatory hush of nature, as the body waited for them to dig its hole. Grady's cheerful sister sitting at the reception desk flashed across his mind. He wouldn't be able to go there again, wouldn't be able to look at her. Jon, remaining methodical, paced the length of the grave and Paul shuddered.

"Cover the head first." Jon started to dig. The earth was soft enough but Paul worked up a sweat in under five minutes, even in the cool night air. He shovelled. They had to beat the sun, get back before daylight. He worked through a blister, using a rag taken from Jon's Jeep to protect his hand, handing a strip to Jon. Hours dragged with only the thump of dirt and the minuscule sounds of small animals passing. They were deep enough that only one could fit in the hole at a time, but when the depth was about waist high, Jon threw his shovel down. "Good enough."

Paul grunted and did the same, taking an end and carrying the body to the grave. When it thudded into the hole, he exhaled heavily and the strength returned to his arms as he began shovelling dirt back in, covering the head first. Part of his speed came from the churning in his stomach; the sooner this was done with the better. "What do we do with the rest of the dirt?"

"Into the water."

Paul nodded and sent another load onto the blue tarp.

*

Dirt was still beneath his nails and the blisters were weeping when Jon pulled into his driveway. Laura's car waited beside the BMW but the house was dark and the same silence from the cabin was waiting for them outside Jon's home. Paul walked to his car and glanced at Jon, who was already halfway to the door.

"What now?"

He shrugged. "Keep going. Get on with my life."

"And Laura?"

"I don't know."

"We shouldn't talk for a few days."

"Yeah."

"I'm going to keep looking for Rachel."

He turned. "I'm sorry, Paul. If I hadn't –"

"I'll find her a different way. I have to go." There was nothing else to say. He wanted to get out of his clothes, to shower; he wanted the hot water to wash away the last few days. He got into his car. Fat chance. They were scoured into his brain and the image of Grady wrapped in a blue tarp, the same tarp he'd once used to protect furniture, was never far. Or the man's foot, visible in the shower of cabin ten in Three Hills Caravan Park. The rustling thump of dirt hitting in regular rhythm, one, two, one two, Jon, Paul, Jon, Paul.

He drove slowly, arriving at Anton's sometime after midnight. He knocked on the door and he rubbed his eyes with the palms of his hands. After a series of clicks and rattling of locks, Anton, looking sleepy himself, appeared in the entryway, Alessandra in tow.

"Paul, you look terrible."

"I'm not hurt." He crouched before Alessandra. "Alessandra, would you like to stay here tonight, with Signor Battisti?"

Anton translated and she nodded. "*Si*, Paul. *Tu vai e dormi.*"

"Go home and sleep?" he asked with a small smile, and Anton nodded.

"That's good advice she's giving you."

"It is. I'll come and collect her tomorrow."

"All right, get home then."

Before he reached Mayfield Drive, Kelly called, and he answered without pulling over, not in the mood for delay.

"Hello, Kelly? I'm so sorry I –"

"Paul," she broke in. "Don't go home, the police are there. There are two cars, a squad car and an unmarked car."

He pulled over. Two cars didn't sound like a visit for further questioning. "Where are you?"

"Home. I've been trying to call you but I couldn't get through till now."

"I...haven't been in service."

"You better come to my place then. Mikey's with his dad."

"Good idea." It was only a temporary solution, but it beat a night in the cell. "Where do you live?"

*

Number twenty seven. Kelly's house was on the other side of town, and turning left at the football oval as per her instructions, he pulled into a dark street lined with shrubs and what seemed like a small park or set of play equipment on every other block. Perfect street for a young family.

He parked behind her small car and knocked on the

door, wren under one arm. It was a newish house, with the look of a display home or something from a catalogue, but it seemed tidy and clean in the dark. The front garden even had a set of winding stone pavers, carefully arranged.

Kelly answered, dressed in a nightshirt and gown, pulling him into a bright entryway.

"I'm sorry. I'm in trouble, Kelly."

"And covered in dirt." She folded her arms, one eyebrow raised. "I guessed something was going on when you stood me up. Again. Listen Paul, I like you but I've had enough –"

"I know, I'm sorry, Kelly. But things have been crazy."

"Come on, Paul. I don't need excuses. Just be honest and..." she trailed off, her voice becoming strained. "What's wrong with that bird?"

He didn't look up. "It's sick. I've been trying to help it."

"But its colour is...it looks see-through."

"I know." He straightened. "Kelly, everything's worse than before, worse than Maddocks and the assault and everything else. I don't know when the police will leave and Rachel is missing and..." He took a breath and stopped. "I need something to drink."

She took him to a stylish kitchen full of pastel tones, from the splashback and taps, to hardware like the electric mixer or the lamp fittings overhead. A plunger and two cups of coffee sat on the kitchen table, where she'd obviously waited for him. Kelly switched on a few more lights and fumbled around in a cupboard a moment, handing him a bottle of bourbon. He placed the bird on the table and took a swig, ignoring the burn. "I think she's pregnant with my baby."

Her eyes widened. "You're sure?"

"I think that's what she wanted to tell me when she came

that night."

"And now she's missing?" Kelly led him to a chair. With his head heavy and his arms aching, he did as directed, slumping down. She cradled his hands, her brow furrowed as she examined the blisters. "What happened to you, Paul? Where have you been?"

"I can't say. You don't need to know. It's safer for you if you don't. If the police find out…"

"Jesus, don't trail-off like that, Paul. Let me help."

"I can't –"

"Bullshit. I'm offering. And I can handle it," she snapped, getting up to shove a glass beneath a tap and handing it to him. "You might even be worth it too."

"Okay, all right." He drank. "Is there a chance I could shower first?"

She looked him up and down. "I guess so. Well, take your time. I'll make us something."

He took another drink. "I'm not really hungry."

"Too bad, I am."

"How long were you waiting?" He searched for a clock.

"Hours, you bastard, now go and clean up."

Paul let Kelly direct him to her impeccably clean and ordered bathroom and into the shower, leaving him with a warning about messing the place up. He washed with slow movements, letting the hot water soak beneath his skin. It soothed his muscles and even though it stung his trembling hands, the torrent of water pouring over his head was bliss. Kelly needed to know what was going on. If he was serious about her he needed to be honest; she needed to know what she was getting involved with. Somehow she'd stuck around through everything else, could she handle murder and magical fairy wrens?

And Rachel. What could he do now? Go to the police? They'd be thrilled to help – help him into a pair of cuffs. Wherever Grady had put her, whatever he'd done, Paul would have to find her alone. She had no-one else.

Paul finished up, grimacing at the touch of his dirty clothes, clothes he'd have to get rid of, and met Kelly at the table. "Ready for a long story?"

He told her everything over their meal. He couldn't say what he'd eaten by the end, sitting there, pushing food scraps around his plate and watching Kelly struggle for words. "Paul, I..." She stood, starting to pace. "Holy shit, Paul. You buried the mayor's son? Where? No, you're right, don't answer that. God, Paul. I don't know what to say. You're mad, you're fucking mad." She turned away. "What the hell have I gotten into?"

"I'm sorry. I wanted you to know everything. To know what you're involved with, you know, give you a chance to get away. Even though I don't want you to."

She didn't seem to have heard him, stopping at the towel. "And the bird, do you really think it spoke through that man? Come on, Paul. I mean, it's freakish how it looks but I just don't –" She stopped, having touched it with her finger. Her face drained of colour and she blinked, snatching her hand away.

"What was that?"

He leant forward, chair creaking. "Kelly, you saw something, didn't you?"

"Oh God, Paul. Tell me everything again."

Chapter 18

Breaking into Stony Bay Real Estate wasn't exactly 'breaking in' Paul decided as he followed Kelly into the dark offices, it was more like ignoring the rules of visiting hours at a hospital, or going backstage without being part of the show. Using her key on the back door and typing the alarm code was simple enough, as was logging into a computer to look up 'Grady Dolan.'

Kelly pointed to the screen. "Just like I said. He owns three properties and two of them are rentals. Grady's own house on Fairview was paid for by daddy, but the other two he got for himself. One's also on Fairview Crescent but the other's out of town a bit."

"And you think Rachel's in one of them?" Half-blinded from the screen's glare, dark shapes around the room became indistinct. Had something moved? No, he was imagining things. He rubbed his eyes then rolled his shoulders. The shower and meal had gone some way to giving him a second wind, but closing in on Rachel was better.

"I do. When I touched the wren, I saw Grady shoving

pills down a woman's throat. It was dark but it was definitely Rachel. She looked pregnant and she started to cry when he left, she was just lying on a bed with only a thin sheet and the light that came through a crack in the blind showed me the wallpaper," Kelly said. "I've seen that wallpaper with the blue and pink teddy-bears before, years ago. I just can't remember which property."

"Makes sense, she's not in Grady's place in Fairview," he said. "What about the rental out of town, it'd be quieter. Is it occupied?"

She clicked again. "No."

"That's good enough for me."

"I'll get the keys; do you know how to get to Jennings Lane?"

"Yes."

It was difficult to follow the speed limit but he managed to keep the wagon on the road. He even slowed a little on the unsealed road that led to Jennings Lane. The gravel under the tyres seemed to contain the roaring voices of a vengeful, classical Greek chorus line, or a pride of lions. Eucalypts loomed, bone-white in the headlights, their leaves still in the night. No glimmers of light came from beyond the trees, residents of any nearby homes were doubtless sleeping.

"Number 204," Kelly said when the painted sign for *one hundred and eighty eight* appeared on their right. Paul kept on, each even number flashing by, until a weathered letterbox with the correct numbering appeared. He spun the wheel and flew through the gates, somehow saving the side mirror from one of the posts and sending Kelly grasping for the dash. "Careful."

"Sorry."

At the end of a curved driveway he ground to a halt. In the high beams an old house crouched between a water tank and a closed shed. A gutter sagged from the corrugated iron roof and the front door was ringed by a garden of native plants. No lights bloomed in the windows. All was silent when he got out of the car, keeping the lights on while Kelly flicked through a set of keys. "Got a torch?"

"In the glovebox. Why?"

She grabbed it. "The power might not be on."

Paul followed her to the door. He tapped his feet while she fitted the key, his teeth clenched as he watched her fumble for a light switch. "Electricity's off," she said over her shoulder, and he accepted the torch, leading her into a hall. A furnished but dusty bedroom stood to the left, then an empty kitchen and a lounge with a portable television, but no sign of Rachel. A bunch of medical supplies were stacked on the sink, bandages and vials and pill boxes whose names he didn't recognise. A packet of gloves rested atop a pile of folded towels. None of the drugs possessed the customary stickers for scripts.

"What's going on?" he hissed.

"A home birth?"

Paul frowned, shining the torch on the pile. "That's not enough, is it? Wouldn't he need more? What sort of drugs do they use?"

"I don't know."

"Come on." He hurried through a doorway beyond the lounge, into a short hall with two more bedrooms.

The first was the room from his vision.

Rachel lay still, chest barely rising and falling, legs and enormous stomach tangled in a thin sheet. Her hair was lank, deep rings surrounded her eyes and she'd been drooling on her singlet and the big pillows. "Rachel." He shook her gently, and though her eyes fluttered, she didn't wake. On a bedside table an empty water bottle stood with a bowl and spoon, along with empty pill packets.

"He's drugged her," Kelly said.

Paul shook her again. "Rachel, wake up." Was she going to be all right? Had the drugs hurt the baby too? He slammed a fist into his thigh as Rachel groaned. "What do we do?"

Kelly already had her phone out. "I need an ambulance to two hundred and four Jennings Lane. There's a woman in labour here." Her voice was steady but she paced in and out of the torchlight. Paul stroked Rachel's hair and found her sweaty hand beneath the sheet, giving it a squeeze. "God, what did he do?" Rachel continued to groan, shifting her legs. Nothing he did made any difference. All he managed was to hold her hand and exchange worried glances with Kelly.

He had no idea how long he'd knelt at the bed when the ambulance finally screamed up the driveway but his limbs were numb. The paramedics burst into the room and he stumbled to his feet to give them space. Kelly was answering all their questions and he'd slumped against the wall. In moments they had Rachel on a stretcher, oxygen mask on, and Kelly was pulling him along, herding him into the passenger seat of his car.

Keeping close behind the ambulance, which cut a path through the light, early morning traffic, they arrived at the mismatched buildings of the hospital before he was able to organise his thoughts. Rachel was rushed to Emergency and he found himself banished to an empty waiting room with its coffee machine and magazines. A nurse arranged Christmas decorations on her desk, hanging tinsel that caught the light.

Kelly led him to a seat. "Thanks." He sat with his head in his hands. "I was pretty useless back there."

"Yes, you were," Kelly said. "But don't worry. She'll be fine. They both will."

"Think so?"

A slight pause. "I do."

He sat straight. "What did they say?"

"Nothing, just to wait. This is the best place for her, Paul." She rested a hand on his knee and he placed his own over it.

"What if –"

"She'll be fine." She kissed his cheek. "Let me get you some coffee. I have to check on Mikey anyway, see if his father's still awake."

"Okay." He leant back in the chair, slouching low and closing his eyes, slipping into an exhausted sleep.

*

Someone shook him awake. In the flat light of early morning, surrounded by white walls and splashes of pamphlet colour, he struggled into a sitting position, muscles cramped. "Paul." Kelly sat at his side and an older man in surgical garb stood before him, his greying hair mostly covered and a pair of glasses low on his nose.

"Mr Fischer, your ex-wife is conscious now. Some of the effects of her sedation have worn off, but you can't see her just yet."

"But she's okay?"

"She will unfortunately suffer some after-effects from

such a prolonged exposure to the sedatives. We estimate that she's been drugged regularly for at least a week, maybe two, so she won't be taking visitors until she's had more time to recover."

He heaved a sigh of relief but stopped halfway through. "And the baby?"

The doctor gave him a look that Paul had seen a hundred times in films and television and it thundered into him with the force of a jet. Face to face, it was crippling. His stomach churned. "No."

"I'm sorry, Mr Fischer. We attempted an emergency C-section but we believe the stress of her ordeal, combined with the drugging might have contributed to the stillbirth. If you would like to see –"

"No!" Paul shot to his feet. The wren would help him, the wren would fix everything. He just had to go and get it, bring it back. It would know what to do. It had to. It helped him with Rachel. It had to.

Kelly stood, reaching out a hand. "Paul, there's nothing –"

"Keys, I need my keys."

"What?"

"And yours, quickly." The doctor was speaking but he paid the man no mind. "The wren, Kelly, hurry."

Kelly pulled them from her bag, hesitating when she saw his expression. Paul snatched them and ran from the waiting room, her cry lost as he tore down the halls, dodging shuffling patients and angry nurses. An exit sign appeared ahead and he homed in on the green blob like a missile, exploding into a staff car park and circling the hospital. Out front he found his wagon, parked between a motorbike and a van.

His mind was focused like a mirror reflecting light as he drove, everything came to him as he needed it. For once, his senses let him stay half a step in front, providing every answer. A car swerved in front of him, he was already slipping into the next lane. A roadwork sign flashed ahead, he was already turning down a side street. The great bulk of a log truck blocked a turn so he took the shoulder, bouncing up the curb and scratching the door, approaching Kelly's house at exactly sixty kilometres an hour and slamming the brakes on to screech into her driveway. Leaving the motor running, he found her house key on the chain and charged inside, kicking at a boot that got in his way. He skidded into the kitchen and grabbed the wren. The bird was completely translucent again, as if the vision it gave Kelly had taken the last of its life.

He refused to acknowledge the way his heart stumbled at the idea. "Come on, little wren. Stay with me."

He had one more stop to make.

This time, Anton's wife Francesca answered the door, and he called for Alessandra before giving Francesca only the briefest greetings. "I'm sorry, it's an emergency. At the hospital," he told her. Alessandra rose from where she worked on a puzzle in the longue room. She took her bag and came to the door.

"Is everything all right?" Francesca asked. Her welcoming smile had fallen. "You look awful, Paul."

"I know. But I won't be long. Alessandra, *pronto, per favore*," he pleaded, waving his arm. She rushed forward and he led her to the passenger seat, where she once again cradled the fairy wren, frowning when she saw it. "Paul!"

"I know."

Again he drove reckless, mad even, but somehow remained untouchable, screeching up to the hospital and double-parking near the entrance. Jumping out of the car, wren in arm, he helped Alessandra out. They'd only taken three steps when she stopped and rushed back to the car. "What's wrong?" he called.

She leapt inside and pulled the trumpet out of her bag.

"Hurry." He didn't question it; she could help. He knew it. She could help.

Inside the bright hospital he charged the front desk, shoes slapping on the linoleum, only slowing at the sight of the receptionist's face. He must have looked desperate, dragging a young girl into the hospital and panting.

"Excuse me, ma'am, but where's the mortuary?"

She leant forward, putting a pen down. "Are you all right, sir?"

"Yes. Please, it's important."

"Ah, it's to the back of the hospital."

"Yes."

She pointed. "You have to take the main hall, then pass the cafeteria on the left. You'll see another nurse's station and they can send you to – wait, don't you want to hear the rest of it?" She shouted the last part as he strode off, Alessandra in tow. He could get more directions closer to the mortuary.

The main hall was lined with patients, nurses and sombre-faced visitors. All were obstacles but he couldn't bring himself to charge through them, despite grinding his teeth whenever they slowed him. A trolley resting against a wall and a wheelchair-bound child held him up at the cafeteria, but their intervention turned into a blessing when he spotted two familiar figures leaving the counter.

Detective Clarke and Constable Stevens were clearly on duty. Uniforms and guns, deep in conversation. They knew about Rachel. The hospital would have called. The police would be watching her room, waiting to talk to her. Waiting for him too. Paul slid back around the corner, pulling Alessandra after him. Clarke's voice grew louder, audible over the general hum. "He'll show. He's already been here once."

"Are you sure?"

"Yeah. Poor guy lost his kid. At the least, he'll be back to see his ex."

Paul kept Alessandra close. She had a question on her face but he held a finger to his lips. They might recognise her too. Nothing could stop him. Not arrest and not questioning, he couldn't waste a minute.

"Quick." He pulled her into a nearby toilet. The door clicked shut and a moment later two pair of heavy tread passed. Paul waited as long as he dared before leaving the ultra-sanitised room and peering into the hallway. The officers were nearly out of sight. He led Alessandra past the cafeteria and down another hall, until coming to a second nurse's station, where a man sent him to a not-too distant blue elevator.

"Finally." He jabbed the 'down' button.

The descent took too long, but when the elevator stopped it opened to a cooler, darker floor and he exhaled. The hall was empty and the only hint of movement came from behind a door at its end. There was a hush here that completely swallowed any sound from the floor above. His breathing was too loud.

Alessandra moved closer. "*Ho paura.*"

"It's all right. Don't be frightened," he said, somehow understanding. Her small hand in his brought a tear to his eye and he wiped it away. He tried to breathe evenly. It had to work. Pushing the door open, he went through and spotted the medical examiner on duty, a short woman with a handful of folders and a mask around her neck.

"Excuse me. I'm here to see the Anderson stillborn." His voice broke on the word. "I'm the father."

Her face softened. "I'm sorry, sir. Do you have identification? I have to ask."

He managed to hand over his old licence and wait without fidgeting while she glanced it over, then checked a nearby computer. She handed it back. "All right, Mr Fischer, come with me." The baby was his; he knew that beyond a doubt now. Rachel or Kelly or the police must have told the hospital as much, otherwise the medical examiner would have turned him away. Paul held back more tears as he followed her to a small shape on a steel slab at the back of the room. Sets of rectangular steel doors covered the back wall and seemed to swallow the light. The soft footsteps of the medical examiner were like whispers. He shivered in the cold, keeping Alessandra close.

"Her skin is fragile, sir," the woman said, pulling back the sheet. The baby girl was dark, bluish, as if not enough oxygen had been given to her. Her eyes were closed and her hands were curled up. No breath stirred in her chest.

Paul flinched but moved closer, his own chest shrinking. "Lord."

"Take as long as you need, Mr Fischer." She glanced at the trumpet and towel before leaving, but made no comment.

Alessandra's eyes were large and he knelt before her, a sob escaping. "Alessandra, can you sing? *Canta?*"

"*Si,*" she whispered then began, her voice quiet.

"To the wren." He pointed to the bird where it nestled in the towel, its home for days now. Alessandra looked down, her voice raising a little. His fists stayed clenched at his sides, one of them seeming to warp the shaft of the trumpet. A swirl of colour moved beneath the wren's wing and Alessandra sang louder. More colour returned, spreading through its head and tail, down to the pale feet. Paul squeezed his eyes shut before checking on his baby. Had she lost some of her colour, was the blue disappearing? His heart lurched. "Keep going." The medical examiner was trying not to watch, busying herself with paperwork at a desk.

Alessandra sang on. He glanced back and forth, bearing witness as the two small bodies traded colours. The wren's feather became a familiar mix of rich black and vibrant blue, tufts of white beneath the wings. One of the tail feathers was like the ocean in the middle of summer, so crisp and with such depth. He sucked a breath. His baby girl had been transformed – she was pink and healthy-looking, her limbs relaxed, the darkness beneath her eyelids gone.

But neither moved as Alessandra trailed off, her face expectant. He reached out a hand but couldn't touch the baby or the bird, caught between both. "Please wake up."

It wasn't enough. He choked back a sob. "What else do you want?" He had no idea who he was speaking to, but he'd been so sure. What went wrong? Neither figure moved and Paul hung his head, pulling at his own hair. "Don't do this. If you can help me, little wren, please."

"*Devi suonarla,*" Alessandra said. She was pointing at the

trumpet, miming that he play it with her free hand.

He raised it. "I can't, I don't know how."

Alessandra began to sing again, the same song, shooting him a look, and he put the trumpet to his mouth and blew. Nothing happened. Alessandra didn't stop. He tried again, changing his lips. A pathetic sound escaped. Paul puffed his cheeks and pressed a valve, squeezing his eyes tight as he blew. Nothing.

Alessandra's sweet voice grew louder. He stopped and just listened a moment, before fitting his lips to the trumpet and depressing a valve. A clear note sounded as he tried to match her voice. An ethereal hand seemed to brush against his own, as he depressed the first valve and found breath for another note, then the second, going higher and lower as Alessandra did. He played without thinking, guided by her voice or the imagined touch of another hand, but he didn't open his eyes, he couldn't risk it. The magic was fragile. He moved his fingers and drew in great breaths to keep up with the young girl, until he felt the song coming to an end, and held his last note.

Please.

Before it finished, before the mortuary swallowed Alessandra's last word, before he opened his eyes, the sounds of birdsong and the cries of a newborn filled the room.

The baby kicked on the table, her face screwed up in surprise. Paul dropped the trumpet. Its clattering seemed to echo a long time. Every muscle in his body relaxed, the tension flowing from his fingertips like an invisible torrent dashing itself on the tiles with just the hint of a sigh. He leant down and scooped up his baby, hands trembling as he smiled at a tearful Alessandra, who smiled back.

Taking his baby's tiny hand and letting her grip his finger he met her blue eyes and she hushed. "Hello there, sweetheart."

The medical examiner rushed over, babbling away beside them, crying about a miracle but Paul couldn't hear her words.

"Come see," he told Alessandra, who stepped forward, placing the cloth-nest on the table then reaching out to stroke his daughter's cheek. Paul blinked.

The towel was empty.

Chapter 19

Finding Rachel's room had been difficult. The woman from the mortuary was torn between helping him bring the baby to her mother and trying to rationalise the miracle. Neither he nor Alessandra mentioned the wren's disappearance, and the medical examiner hadn't seemed to notice. It wasn't until Paul let her examine the fussing baby that the woman agreed to take him there.

"Did you massage her, was that it?"

"I'm not sure."

"I can't believe…I mean…Mr Fischer, it's a miracle. There's no other word for it." Her mouth was a little slack but she led them on, shaking her head as they moved deeper into the recovery ward. Unlike other hospitals, the Stony Bay Health Complex was not decorated by pastel paintings or landscapes and other inoffensive subject matter, but vibrant colours and scenes from all aspects of life, paintings with outlines, having almost the look of cartoons. Naive Art, he plucked the name from his memory, pleasing himself. Today, such a small victory was titanic.

Today he could have swallowed the sun with a hiccup and smiled sunbeams.

Rachel was slumped in cool white sheets, propped up by pillows. Her hand sported a drip and staff had made some effort to clean her up. She still looked weak, gaunt even, but her eyes opened as he came in, Alessandra and nurse in tow. It took her a moment to focus, and when she did her jaw dropped.

"Rachel. Something unbelievable's happened."

"Paul?"

He handed over the bundle. "This is our daughter."

Rachel's shoulders trembled but she cradled the baby, tears streaming down her face. "But the doctors told me she died," she choked out. "I wanted to see her, after, after they took her away. I tried."

"They say it can happen sometimes." Paul ignored the look the medical examiner gave him. "But she's all right now."

"Oh Sasha, Mummy's here."

Sasha. The name they'd chosen when–

"He's here, sir."

A voice shattered the moment.

Constable Stevens stood in the doorway, one hand on the butt of his weapon. "Ma'am, young lady, please stand aside. Mr Fischer, place your hands on your head and turn around."

"Paul, what's happening?" Rachel shielded the baby with her arms. Alessandra stepped in front of Paul and the medical examiner froze, glued to the spot.

"Ma'am, little girl, please. This is police business."

"It's all right." Paul raised his hands. His sun set in his

stomach, hissing and bubbling. At least he got to see Rachel safe and meet his daughter. Sasha. "Please, I'm not going to make trouble, but can we do this outside? I don't want to frighten my baby and Rachel has been ill."

The policeman glanced at Rachel, but did not move forward. Footsteps approached and Detective Clarke joined them, his cuffs ready. "Do as Owen said."

Paul turned slowly. To the medical examiner he said, "Can you take Alessandra to Kelly Wilson? She'll be in the emergency waiting room I think."

The woman nodded as someone cuffed him with curt efficiency. The same person seemed to be reading him his rights but it was static. How could he explain what was happening to Alessandra? Her eyes flicked from face to face and she was asking Paul questions but he couldn't answer. Rachel had added her own voice to the clamour.

"Find someone who can speak Italian, explain to Alessandra that I'll be back," he said, looking at the medical examiner then Rachel, as he was pulled to the door.

"Paul, what's going on?"

"Everything will be all right," he shouted from the hall, and her reply was lost as once again, someone demanded to know if he'd understood his rights.

"I do."

*

Lloyd Dahl shuffled into the jail, sitting on a stool before the bars. As ever, he wore a tie that screamed 'yellow' – today it was painfully lemon. He removed his glasses, placing them in an inner pocket of his jacket and opening his briefcase. He didn't bother with a greeting. "What time is it, Paul?"

"Eleven o'clock in the morning, Lloyd."

"I may make dinner after all."

"What do you mean?"

"Wait until you see this list of charges."

"That long?"

"That long. I fear I will need to hire an associate to cover my other clients for a while."

Paul sighed. "So Rachel agreed to give a statement?"

"She did, so you might expect some leeway from Senior Detective Clarke – nothing official, mind, so we shall see. Of course, Rachel will not claim that her intervention order has been violated, saving her life turned out to be a good move – legally and from a humanist standpoint. For once, good show."

"Appreciate that, Lloyd."

"Congratulations on becoming a father, by the way." He gave a fleeting smile. "I also found the trumpet you asked about, Ms Wilson has it. Now to business. I know the police will get you on something, and the assault charges for Maddocks are proving to be quite persistent for one."

"Can't be helped, I suppose."

Lloyd frowned. "Paul, this is adding up to jail time, did you know that?"

"Yeah."

"Well, all that aside," Lloyd waved his hands, dismissing Paul's calm, "your fatalism is not helping. Take this seriously, you are in trouble, do you hear me, boy? Trouble with a capital Go-to-Prison-for-a-Long-Time."

"I know."

"Do you?" The old man glared at him, jaw set. "I promised your father, Paul. I promised him, do you understand?"

An image of his father in the hospital flashed; his once powerful forearms thin and wasted where they rested above the sheet and Mum looking out the window, her knuckles white where they held his hand. "I'm sorry, Lloyd. I'll do my best."

The man gave a grunt.

"Do you know what the police found out about Grady? No-one's talking to me."

"Not much yet, but for drugging and holding a woman prisoner, I know they are looking for him. They seem very, very interested in talking to him."

"But why, Lloyd – what was he doing with her out there in Jennings Lane?"

"That I do not know. Perhaps ask Rachel?"

"I will. As soon as I'm out of here."

"Well, it is gratifying to see you setting goals. Let us go to work then."

*

Jon drove him home after making bail that evening. He was getting to know the officers at the charge counter pretty well. When they pulled into Paul's driveway, Jon cut the engine and hesitated before speaking. "Thank you, Paul."

"I should be thanking you."

He shook his head. "Don't worry about that. And I'm real glad Rachel is okay, and your kid too."

He grinned. "I have to keep reminding myself it's real."

"Yeah. It's good, Paul. It's good," he mumbled.

"Jon, are you all right? With…"

"No."

Paul waited.

"I see him a lot. His face. How it looked after. When I'm in a meeting, when I take a leak – shit, even when I look at Laura. Every time I look at her." He was breathing a little hard and he leant back in the seat. "I really can't sleep, Paul."

"Have you tried sleeping pills?"

"I could but how am I supposed to stop thinking about it in the day?"

"Focus on good things?" It sounded pathetic. "I don't know. I can still see him, in the hole. It feels wrong, Jon. But...I know what he was planning to do to Rachel and my daughter. What he *did* do to them. And that helps me. I know what he was," Paul said.

"Yeah."

"Are things better between you and Laura?"

"Dunno. She's quieter, it's not right. She can tell I know about her and Grady. But neither of us talk. We watch television, or eat in separate rooms. I haven't seen her for breakfast since before it happened. Sometimes it's like she's going to tell me something, then she rushes into the kitchen and starts cooking. Stuff she hasn't cooked for years, extravagant stuff."

"She loves to cook –"

"The other day I found plane tickets in her name; she was going to go to Bali. With him probably."

Paul closed his mouth, whatever he'd been going to say forgotten.

"It was from weeks ago. Before I knew about Grady, but she never took it."

"Wait, wasn't it your anniversary about then?"

"I guess so."

"She still loves you. I'm sure of it."

He turned, and his eyes were red-rimmed. In the police station Paul hadn't really noticed, getting out had been so damn good, especially after the 'pep talk' from Lloyd. "Maybe. That's what I want to believe but I don't know anymore. The dates on the tickets, I can't remember if they match up with our anniversary." He rubbed his thighs.

"She loves you, Jon."

He nodded to himself. "I got rid of the shovels, I'll buy you new ones. I think I should sell the Jeep too."

"We wrapped the tarp tight enough. There won't be anything in the Jeep."

"I guess. I heard from Three Hills. They're charging me for the damage to the cabin, but they haven't mentioned anything else. I did a pretty good job of cleaning up. Best I've ever cleaned anything. Laura would be surprised." He gave a weak laugh.

"Maybe you should talk to someone, like a counsellor? Just leave out the stuff about what happened in the cabin." It sounded stupid, very stupid, Paul knew. "Talk about Laura."

"Maybe."

"Has Clarke been to see you about the disappearance of Grady?"

"Yeah, twice. I told him I don't know anything – I can handle him, Paul. It's Laura who's the problem. I don't know what to do. Our marriage is over."

"You haven't tried talking to her yet. You should. And if you think it's over already, you don't have anything to lose by trying."

Jon stared into the dark street. "Yeah. Yeah. Thanks, Paul. I'll let you get home, bet you're hungry."

"I am a bit. Thanks for the lift." Paul got out of the car.

"Thanks, Paul," he said as he started the engine.

Jon would be all right if he had Laura's support. He loved her too much to survive otherwise – Paul would watch him anyway. He waved and went inside where he slumped over the kitchen bench and stared, seeing nothing. When he finally got up it was to make a microwave meal, throw his clothes in the bin and shower, before collapsing across his bed. The sheets were soft and his pillow cradled his head in loving arms of feather and fabric, and just before he fell asleep, he curled into the foetal position.

Chapter 20

Rachel's hospital room receded as baby Sasha took up the whole of his attention where she lay in his arms. "She's so small," he said, and missed Rachel's reply when the baby yawned, eyelids closing. Paul swallowed. Was she the wren? Had her spirit taken flight to try and warn him that mother and babe were in danger? It wasn't hard to believe, after everything he'd seen the fairy wren do, after what it had known and after what it helped him do. No way to know, but maybe it didn't matter.

"Paul, the nurse needs to take her," Rachel said. Her tone was a little exasperated, as if she'd been talking for a while. The nurse smiled at him, holding out her arms. "We just need to make sure her mother gets some rest, Mr Fischer. So don't you keep her too long."

He handed Sasha over. "I won't."

Rachel laughed. "You're obsessed already."

"True." He watched the nurse take Sasha out.

"I never got to thank you properly, you know," Rachel said, looking away.

He moved the chair closer to the bed. Her skin colour was returning to normal, and the rings beneath her eyes were fading – all good signs. "Well, I was being arrested at the time so you're off the hook."

"Idiot."

"So, do you want to talk about it?"

"Maybe."

She didn't continue and he waited, but Rachel had a glazed look in her eye, she was rubbing her thighs, hands making a gentle 'swooshing' sound. "Is he gone?"

"I think so," Paul said. He hesitated. "The police will catch him."

Rachel said nothing.

"Did you try and call me, weeks and weeks ago, at the store?" he tried.

"I thought...Grady was scaring me and I thought you could help," she finished in a rush. "I was going to tell you about the pregnancy."

Paul opened his mouth but his mind was an empty hive.

"He wanted me out of the way until he could figure out what to do with the baby," she added when he made no sound. "Those last couple of weeks I didn't know up from down, Paul. I just, I knew I was in trouble."

"That place in Jennings Lane had some medical supplies in the kitchen. It looked like he wanted to have a home birth."

She nodded. "So he could do something to the baby." Her expression darkened. "God, the bastard. When he found out she wasn't his, he was furious, he *demanded* I have an abortion." She squeezed back tears, wiping at her eyes and laying her head back in the pile of pillows. Paul took her hand. "Maybe he wanted to lie, and say I'd had a miscarriage or that something went wrong during the birth? I don't know if I'd have known any different, Paul. I was out of it." She heaved a sigh. "I'm just glad you got there in time."

Listening to her speak, there was not a single cell in his body that was sorry the man was dead in a hole. "He sounds crazy."

"He was. While we argued about the abortion, nothing I said made a difference, he just kept ranting about 'betrayal' and how he wouldn't raise a bastard as his own."

"Betrayal, my arse. He was sleeping with Laura." Paul stopped. "Oh, Rach, I'm sorry."

"No, it's fine. I knew."

"You did?"

"I found out just before all this started. Remember when I came over and you had your friend there? Kelly? She came to see me before, she's nice."

"Yeah, she is."

"That was right after I found out about Laura, I was going to ask you about it and tell you I was pregnant, that the baby was yours. I should have stayed, I was so god-damn stupid. I shouldn't have kept it from you. I'm sorry, Paul."

"Don't worry about any of that now."

"No, I am stupid. Grady sucked me in, totally. He was charming, handsome, well-off, he had it all, right? I should have left him after he threw me round that first time."

"You're too dependent," he said softly.

"So you kept telling me. But I didn't listen then. Or after Grady hit me."

"You came to me instead."

She shrugged. "Maybe I shouldn't have. I was just looking

for comfort. I never thought we'd end up in bed, Paul."

He raised an eyebrow. "Really? I mean, you'd just slapped the intervention on and then you showed up crying for me to hold you."

"Really, Paul. I was scared, I thought I'd made a big mistake with Grady and just wanted to talk. It didn't help that he seemed really sincere when he apologised the next day."

"Was he that convincing?"

"Yes."

"That's hard to believe."

Her eyes flashed. "Well he was, Paul, okay? Can you just –"

"Sorry."

He poured a drink from the glass jug, which had been placed beside her bed, offering her a cup. She shook her head and he drank. "So you gave him another chance."

"Yeah. It was good for a while after, for months actually, but it didn't last. Once we found out I was pregnant, he made me take a paternity test. I refused at first – some of them are dangerous, but it made him more suspicious, and once the results came in..."

"He lost control."

She nodded. "I came to see you, but once I left I made the mistake of going back to get my things. He was waiting for me, and he was very calm. I should have seen it then, but I sat down and had a drink. Told him I'd talk it out. He said he didn't care who the father was. Not that it mattered, I mean, without a sample from you, he'd never have found out anyway."

"He couldn't guess? I mean, you never talked about me?"

"Not really. I was trying to deny you existed when I met Grady, and it was after I moved out of Mum and Dad's."

Paul gave a wry smile. "So the drink was drugged?"

"It had to have been; I don't remember anything about the rest of the night. When I woke I was in that place."

"Jennings Lane. Do you know how long you were there?"

"No. It's hard to put it together; it's still in fragments. But that first time, I saw a bit of light from the window and I could see through, into bushland." She rubbed at her wrist. "I tried to get out but I couldn't do it. I didn't have a phone or anything. I don't know how long it was before he came again. I think I'd already fallen asleep from exhaustion."

"Did he ever say anything? About why he was doing it?"

"No. It didn't matter what I said to him when I could actually speak, he just forced the pills down my throat, made sure I'd swallowed them and left."

"Well, don't worry about him now," Paul said.

"I don't know, Paul. The police think he's on the run, they can't find him. What if he comes back?"

"He won't."

"How can you be sure?"

"I don't know, but I am. Just trust the police, they'll track him down."

"They'd better," she growled.

Paul smiled, but it faded a little as they kept talking, discussing her father's return and everything the doctors told her about recovery. It wasn't because he had to lie about Grady, but because spending even a small amount of time together was enough to realise he wasn't in love with her anymore. There was no rush, not like when he saw Kelly. Fondness, yes, and some sort of love, or care at least, but they had no future beyond Sasha. Which would be complicated. He'd probably stopped loving her before she went missing, before he met Kelly. It was part fear, part duty, part whatever, that compelled him to help her. He hadn't resented it, his Uncle or Toshiro would have said it was who he was. That he could no more have turned his back on her than chop off his own head.

"Paul, what's wrong? You've drifted off again."

"I was just thinking about us." He stood and moved to the foot of the bed. "Things have changed with me, you know?"

"I know. You've moved on at last."

"Yes."

"That's good, Paul. It's the best thing for both of us." She trailed off with a sigh.

Her eyelids were drooping and he smiled. "I'll let you rest."

"I'm sorry, I'm just so tired, Paul."

"Don't worry. I'll see you tomorrow."

She nodded and he slipped from the room.

Chapter 21

A casually dressed Kelly waited on his doorstep the next morning, a package in hand. Alessandra stood beside her, carrying the trumpet.

"Here's your mail, Paul."

After another restful night, he was impressed that he'd managed to sleep till morning two nights running; some small things were getting back in order. He'd even managed to answer a few e-mails from customers and make plans for another mail-out. Mrs Greenhorne had also visited, offering her congratulations and dropping off an apple pie along with a CD of Eddie's songs.

"It's wonderful news, you must let me see her. Sasha, isn't it? I heard from Susan Alberts at the post office, her husband works at the hospital you see."

"I see."

"A beautiful name, Sasha. And Rachel must be moving home then?"

"No, Mrs Greenhorne. We'll remain divorced, but it's probably for the best."

"Oh. Divorce?" She frowned. "Do you think so?"

"Yes. We don't make each other happy anymore."

Mrs Greenhorne gave him a small smile. "Ah. I see. Well, not everyone figures that out, Mr Fischer, perhaps you can console yourself with that. And Ms Wilson too, perhaps? Do enjoy your pie," she'd said, and reached out to pat his hand, hesitantly at first, but her grip was firm before she left to call for Pebbles.

Launching herself from the doorstep, Alessandra threw her arms around Paul's waist and babbled away in Italian, he caught only a word or two, but he hugged her back. "I'm glad to see you too," he smiled.

Accepting the square package, hopefully a Coltrane CD he'd ordered before the recent madness, he led them both to the kitchen where he prepared a second breakfast with the last of whatever food he could gather. "I'm surprised there's enough for the three of us." He hadn't been shopping properly in weeks. "Haven't you got work?" he asked Kelly as they finished up.

She laughed. "I've got someone covering me. I called in sick the other day and I'm taking some leave."

"Oh, thank God." He shook his head. "It just hit me. I've been pretty selfish when it comes to your time."

Kelly snorted as she collected the plates. "Don't be stupid, it's been a crazy few weeks." She paused. "But yeah, you kinda have. But I forgive you."

"Thanks."

"So what's going to happen to her?" Kelly glanced at Alessandra while they cleaned up, sharing the sink. The girl sat at the piano, playing softly. She was good too; he shouldn't have been surprised. "Has her father come round again?"

"Not that I've seen." He submerged a plate. "If the Department gets involved, hopefully someone else can help. Maybe her mother, wherever she is."

"Oh, I've been meaning to tell you. Anton said Anita died about the time they came to Australia. That's about all he could get out of her on the subject though. Poor girl."

"Oh." He watched Alessandra play the piano, her small face set in concentration. "No wonder she's so protective of that photo."

"Can we ask Anton to help?"

"It's worth a shot."

She stopped a moment. "Paul, I've been meaning to talk to you about something." He opened his mouth to reply but she stalled him, holding up a soapy spoon. "I know things have to change, now that Rachel's safe and you have your little girl, but I want you to know that I liked being with you. I think we could work. I have Mikey after all – I like kids, you know?"

"Yeah?"

"Yeah. And that's even though we haven't really spent that much time doing regular things together, since you're obviously a career criminal." She lost her faint smile. "Even knowing what happened, even with the burden of that secret...I think if you can manage to stay out of prison, I'd like to keep seeing you." Kelly delivered the last of the speech in a rush and he took her dripping hand when she finished.

"Kelly, I have to tell you something too. I wish I hadn't dragged you into everything. I do. And I want to be involved in Sasha's life, but I'm not in love with Rachel. I guess I haven't been for a long time. I figured it out for myself yesterday at the hospital. And I'd like to see you some more too. And meet Mikey, if you want me to?"

She grinned and flicked water at him.

*

Rachel's colour was better and she'd smiled when he walked in, but once again, he found himself mesmerised by his daughter. She was crying and fussing, but he stroked her fine hair until a nurse came and handed her to Rachel for a feeding. He looked away. "Should I go?"

"No, it's fine," Rachel said, sounding distracted.

"All right." He didn't turn around until the nurse left, by which time Sasha was feeding.

"Paul." She paused. "Are you upset? That I got pregnant?"

He frowned. "No, why?"

"Because I tried to. With Grady. But not with you."

He flushed. "Rachel, I –"

"No, don't be angry. Paul, you need to hear this. I wanted to say it yesterday. I tried to say it a long time ago. It wasn't that I didn't want a child at all. It's that I didn't want one with you. You were changing, Paul." She rushed on when he opened his mouth. "You were becoming so cynical, so negative. In our last year together, I couldn't believe it. At Christmas, you barely smiled the whole time, and you love Christmas!"

He tried again but she shook her head. "Let me finish. You became a different person. It was like the joy had been sucked out of you or something. You couldn't see it and I couldn't do that to a child, to stay with you if you were like that. Do you understand?"

Paul stood, turning to the wall. She was right.

"It was like you couldn't change, like you couldn't even try."

"I know."

"I'm sorry, Paul. I don't want to upset you. Maybe I shouldn't dump all this on you right now. Are you all right?" Her face was concerned.

"No, I'm fine."

"Good. Because there's something else. I've been thinking about moving away, for a while now. This might be the best chance."

He flinched. "What do you mean? Where would you go?"

"I don't know yet, but away from...here. From everything that happened."

"But –"

"Dad still lives here. I'll visit, Paul. And you'll always be her father. Besides, I don't even know when I'll go. But I wanted you to know I'm thinking seriously about it."

Fighting her was useless. What he wanted was whatever turned out to be best for Sasha. Right now, that was Rachel, who had Alan's support at least. Paul had nothing but debt, a probable jail sentence and uncertainty. But even if Rachel moved overseas, he would find a way to see his daughter. "I want to be part of her life."

"You will be."

*

Paul walked a festive Shell Street with its green and red Christmas decorations, carrying along a tangled ball of emotions like an invisible pet. It tugged on him, first this way, then that. The Shelob-strength-web of legal troubles was heavy, while his comparative freedom was light. That such freedom might not last was tempered by the knowledge that his daughter was safe and that he had Kelly.

He ducked in to see Teddy and a few other retailers to let them know he was all right. Thanking Anton for helping with Alessandra was important too. She was staying with him until the police could locate her father, something no-one was happy about, though the baker was trying to explain to her that the Department of Human services would not support the man if he was abusive. And Paul would step in himself, if he had to.

Pushing on the door to the bakery, he let the smell of fresh bread and pastries assail him, breathing deep a moment. It didn't take long for Anton to spot him over the heads of an elderly couple.

"Paul, come out back." The man waved him round the counter, leaving the register to one of his sons, Marco. His backroom was part storage, part makeshift office. A small desk was the key feature, which Anton leant on as he turned the radio down. Paul could still hear 'Santa Claus is Coming to Town' as performed by the Jackson 5. "I've been trying to find a way to prove that Alessandra's father is bad news. It's hard to get much out of her, but she trusts you more, Paul. Can you try and get her to show you her bruises? Maybe photograph them?"

"They might have faded, but I'll try."

"I know. Wish I'd been able to see you rough him up."

He grinned. "I restrained myself, Anton. Which wouldn't happen again."

"Well even if the bruises are old now, it could still be useful when DHS come tomorrow."

"All right, I'll do what I can. Can you teach me how to

ask her?"

"Of course. Just remember to open your mouth wide, all right?"

Once Anton was sure he had it close enough, he sent Paul on his way with a sweet pastry, but not before stopping him at the door. "Paul, whatever it was you and Jon were up to, I don't want to know, all right?"

"I understand. Thank you, Anton. Does Alessandra –"

"I don't know. That's one more thing she won't really talk about."

"Good." He took a bite. The custard filling was amazing. "That's for the best, I think. Thanks for looking after her."

"Just remember to talk to her, all right?"

"I will," he promised as he left, giving Marco a wave.

Paul ate as he walked, licking his fingers when he was done and dropping the paper bag in a rubbish bin – which had also been painted green and red. Even the waste disposal arm of the council was on board with the merriment.

Whatever Alessandra had guessed about Grady wasn't likely to come out; she seemed more than able to keep a secret. Nor had it made her afraid of him, so whether she truly knew anything or not, he didn't want to find out. And without her the wren would never have come back to life and nor would Sasha. Alessandra's intelligence and intuition went beyond that of a typical twelve year old – even without the wren's help, she seemed magical all by herself.

He blinked, having stopped at his old store. According to the new signage, resting above the door and painted in the front window, lettered gold and black, Stony Bay Books was now *La Douce*. A groan escaped. He couldn't help it, the name was too much, but he went in anyway. Cocteau and Sanford had managed to make what could have been a spacious café into a crowded place, packing customers in so that when the waitress led him to a table by the window, he bumped into two chairs. The patrons, the place was about half full, didn't really notice, perhaps used to the cramped conditions.

"What can I get you?" The young woman, who once, long ago it seemed, frequented Stony Bay Books, sounded awfully bored.

"Coffee please. Latte."

She flounced off and he let his eyes slide over the new interiors, slick sculptures and prints of European cities at night, their cobblestones gleaming. The counter was now covered in a plain white sheathing with a small payment station and beside it, covering the wall where his crime section once stood, was a long display case of focaccias and cakes. This was presided over by none other than William Cocteau himself, his woollen vest covered by a neat black apron with desperately natural-looking lettering that proclaimed both his and the store's delightful names.

Paul let the chatter of customers blend into an impersonal murmur and simply sat, revelling in the stillness in his head. The walls were the same, he knew his store no matter its façade. He could almost hear the gentle sound of covers sliding against each other as someone pulled a book free of the shelf.

"What are you doing here, Fischer?"

Martin Roberts and the Grinch stood before his table, their suits of a likeness and their expressions equally unpleasant.

"Waiting for coffee."

Maddocks sneered. "I hope it's on the house. You should be saving your money for our little court date, shouldn't you?" They found their own table and Paul smiled, waiting for his coffee to arrive. He took his time finishing it, before getting up and standing before the two.

Roberts frowned. "Go away, Fischer. Unless you want –"

"Shut up, Martin," Paul said pleasantly, "shut up right now. I'm not interested in your blustering. I've brought you something. Actually, it's for both of you." He withdrew a piece of paper and placed it in front of them.

"What's this?"

"Read it and see. It's not much, but it's something interesting, don't you think? I was going to drop it in later, actually. But it's such a nice surprise seeing you here that I thought I'd hand it over now. See your reaction."

Martin's face went red. He scrunched the paper up, making to jam it into a pocket but Maddocks reached for it. Paul made a tut tut sound. "Not to worry, I've got a few copies." He produced another. "I think I might post this around town. Shell Street looks a bit bland, even with the Christmas decorations."

"How did you get this e-mail?" Martin hissed.

"Turns out hacking into a computer through its wireless isn't that hard. You should maybe have a chat with your IT guy."

"This isn't admissible in court."

"I bet the paper would admit it. How's page one sound?"

Maddocks swore at Roberts, and the two broke into a heated argument as Paul drifted away. Who knew what weight it would carry? It wouldn't make Maddocks drop the assault charges but it might have impacted on Martin's aggressive eviction. In any event, Lloyd liked it. The old man had rubbed his hands together, and Paul didn't see the harm in using it to stir them up now.

He strolled the streets of Stony Bay, the smell of the ocean almost hidden beneath car fumes, a smile on his face that had little to do with the warm sun or green leaves. The future was just as uncertain as ever but there was a spring in his step that had everything to do with the fact – tomorrow was nothing like it used to be.

Acknowledgements

A lot of people helped me get *The Fairy Wren* out into the world and I definitely owe them for it. I won't forget how hard you worked either!

First and foremost, my wife Brooke, whose tireless advice and support has not flagged over twelve wonderful years together and whose hard work improved *The Fairy Wren* in so many ways. To both my families who always urge me on, to my writing group the Alchemists (Tess, CJ & Rebekah) whose input was irreplaceable and to the many folks at Scrib who gave their advice too, especially Eliza, Chris, Aderyn and Audreyanna.

Also to Amanda J Spedding for helping me improve the story beyond what I thought was my best, and to David Schembri for making sure the formatting was spot on.

And finally, to Rebekah once again, for such a stunning cover!

Ashley

About Ashley

Ashley is a poet, novelist and teacher living in Australia. Aside from reading and writing, Ashley loves volleyball, Studio Ghibli and *Magnum PI*, easily one of the greatest television shows ever made.

You can find him online at @Ash_Capes or on his fiction blog, www.cityofmasks.com and at www.ashleycapes.com for poetry.

Fiction
The Bone Mask Trilogy
1. *City of Masks*
2. *The Lost Mask* (forthcoming)
3. *Greatmask* (forthcoming)

Poetry
old stone (forthcoming)
between giants
orion tips the saucepan
stepping over seasons
pollen and the storm

www.ingramcontent.com/pod-product-compliance
Lightning Source LLC
Chambersburg PA
CBHW021010120726
47905CB00009B/2948